WHEN THE TIDE GOES OUT

By P J Bennett

To

Sue

Best wishes

Pete Bennett

In Memory of
Maurice and Katia Krafft

Chapter 1

The Observatorio del Roque de los Muchachos,
La Palma, The Canary Islands.

Day 1
11:00 p.m.

As the dense fog of unconsciousness slowly began to lift and then clear, Antonio's befuddled brain fought desperately to make sense of where he was and how he'd got there. The cool marble tile pressing against his right cheek suggested that he was lying on a floor; but which floor and why was he lying there? Antonio tried to get up, but something heavy and immovable was pinning him to the floor. As he struggled to free himself, he was suddenly gripped by a searing pain in the small of his back and waves of dizziness and nausea swept over him.

   With his breathing shallow and laboured Antonio tried to focus on his immediate surroundings. To his left he could just about make out what appeared to be a large white metal cylinder attached to a huge circular mirror and in an instant he remembered that he was in the Observatorio del Roque de los Muchachos, at the top of a volcanic ridge known as Cumbre Vieja.

   Antonio coughed and the excruciating pain racked his body once more. There was a strong metallic taste in his mouth and as he coughed again his blood-flecked spittle was clearly visible on the white polished marble floor. Bracing himself in anticipation of another wave of agonising pain, Antonio tried to move his legs. But strangely the pain didn't come – and his legs didn't move. Questions began to race through his mind with the speed of an express train. Why couldn't he move his legs? Why couldn't he feel them? What had happened to him?

As he fought desperately to control the feelings of panic and fear coursing through his body, he gradually began to recall what had happened. He could remember that he had been standing at the top of the metal spiral staircase which linked the ground floor of the observatory to the telescope's operating platform when suddenly he had begun to sway from side to side, as if he were being pulled one way and then the other by some invisible and irresistible force. He could also recollect having to grab the metal handrail of the staircase in order to stop himself from falling and had a vague memory of the staircase making a low groaning noise. And strangest of all he remembered hearing what sounded like rifle shots and bullets, or something metal at least, ricocheting around the room. After that his mind was a complete blank. Presumably the staircase must have collapsed and the rifle shots could only have been the staircase's rivets and retaining bolts shearing off as it was torn from its wall fixings. Then he must have fallen the twenty or so feet to the floor below where he was now trapped, face down, by several hundred weight of mangled steel and fractured concrete.

Antonio coughed again and the white marble floor against which his face was pressed became a little redder. He was clearly seriously injured and needed help urgently. His eyes scanned the blood splattered floor in front of him, searching desperately for his mobile phone which he had been using as he climbed the stairway to the telescope's gantry, but he couldn't see it anywhere. He knew that unless he could find it, the chances of someone coming to his aid were just about zero as the observatory was unmanned after

7:00 p.m. and he had only been there in order to conduct some over-night maintenance work.

Just as he was about to give up on his visual quest a familiar sound drew his attention to a small pile of buckled steel and broken concrete that lay about two metres to his right. There, not quite buried by the debris, was his phone, manically vibrating and rotating like a child's clockwork toy and with each vibration the pulsating, pale blue light of the phone's key pad could be seen reflected in the pieces of shiny stainless steel that surrounded it. Antonio knew immediately who was calling; it would be his wife asking why he was still at work. He stretched out his right arm in the direction of the phone but instantly realised that it was well beyond his grasp. In his desperation to reach the phone and hear the comforting sound of his wife's voice he tried to move his body closer, but was unable to do so and was punished for his attempt by another sickening wave of pain crashing over him. In spite of the unbearable pain, his eyes remained focused on the wafer thin piece of black plastic that would almost certainly save his life - if only he could get close enough to grasp it. But as the vibrating phone fell silent and the pale blue light of the key pad stopped pulsating, he closed his eyes and lowered his head in acceptance that his best chance of survival had now gone.

His only other hope now was that if the telescope had been damaged by the collapsing staircase. Then, possibly, someone might be sent to investigate the problem. But in his heart Antonio knew that this was unlikely as the scope seemed completely untouched and probably was still functioning as normal.

Antonio let out a small groan as the pain in his spine reached new heights of intensity and the light in the room suddenly became less bright, as if the sun had gone behind a cloud. He lifted his head up as far as he could so as to see which window the light was shining through, but then slowly lowered it again when he remembered that there were no windows in this room; only solid, white, mortuary like, marble walls. As the light in the room seemed to dim a fraction more, Antonio could hear the gurgling sound of fluid in his lungs and with his next cough the scarlet flecks on the white marble floor were transformed into a single pool of thick, dark brown blood.

With his breathing becoming increasingly shallow and as each inhalation became progressively more difficult to accomplish, a high pitched ringing noise began to fill his head. Antonio's vision suddenly began to blur and then slowly faded away until he could no longer see his surroundings. But he could still see - in his mind's eye at least. A picture of his beautiful wife on their wedding day suddenly appeared and then was quickly replaced by one of his parents. Image after image began to race through his mind at break neck speed, almost as if he had pressed the fast forward button on a video player; his children, his first day at school, his first kiss, the birth of his daughter and then suddenly, as if the pause button had been pressed, the images stopped appearing and all that he could see was a single spot of blindingly bright, white light; the sort of light you would see if you closed your eyes after staring at the sun on a hot summer's day. But in the next instant the light began to grow fainter and then fainter still and soon he found himself in a world of total, utter and endless blackness.

Amidst the debris the phone began to vibrate again, but Antonio was no longer aware of its existence and before it had ceased vibrating for a second time, his laboured and shallow breathing had stopped too.

Chapter 2

The Village of San Andres, El Heirro.
The Canary Islands.

Day 2
1:00 a.m.

Maria Gonzales awoke suddenly and sat bolt upright in her bed. Beads of perspiration glistened on her forehead and as she gazed around, momentarily unable to make sense of where she was or how she had got there, she could feel her heart beating rapidly and in time with her equally fast and shallow breathing. Then, as her eyes adjusted to the darkness of her bedroom, familiar objects began to take shape. Her dressing table, her faded red dressing gown hanging on the back of the bedroom door, a pile of discarded clothes on a wooden chair next to her bed gradually came into focus and a feeling of reassurance and relief began to flood through her taut body. The realisation that she was at home, safe in her bed and not, as she had dreamt, in a shaking and rattling railway carriage hurtling along at great speed, was instantly soporific. And within no more than a minute, her eyes had begun to close and she was soon asleep once more; completely oblivious to the bedroom lights being turned on all over the village and the sound of a church bell, clanging incessantly in the stillness of the night.

As Maria sank deeper and deeper into a now dreamless sleep, she was also totally unaware of the growing mayhem all around her. When the church bell eventually stopped its relentless tolling another, more disturbing sound, took its place. It was the distant sound of sirens, gradually becoming louder and louder as the emergency services converged on the small village of San Andres.

Soon the village's streets were filled with people, dressed only in their nightwear and clearly confused and anxious about what had so abruptly woken them from their sleep. Some stood in silence, too shocked to talk. Others cried unashamedly and several, with their faces turned towards the now silent village church, crossed themselves repeatedly and silently mouthed prayers of gratitude to God for delivering them from evil.

Within minutes the previously dark and silent plaza had become a cauldron of noise and a kaleidoscope of colour with the lights of the emergency vehicles reflecting off the windows of the plaza's shops and cafés and illuminating the worried faces of the villagers who had now huddled together in small groups, more for comfort and reassurance than for warmth.

A senior officer from the local fire service was barking out orders to the waiting crews and calling for calm from the village population. In the centre of the plaza, next to the village fountain, a police searchlight was scanning the first and second floor windows of the buildings surrounding it. Fire fighters with axes in hand stood by, primed for action and paramedics, with their gurneys at the ready, waited alongside them. Their eyes followed the beam of the searchlight as it moved from building to building, looking for a sign of anything unusual or untoward.

As the searchlight beam fell momentarily on Maria's bedroom window it flooded her room with bright yellow light, almost as if the dawn had suddenly and instantaneously broken. But Maria remained in a deep, deep sleep. Had she woken she would have no doubt noticed that the photograph of her family, which had hung on the wall above her bed for more years than she could recall, was now no longer there. Nor was the tumbler of water which she had carefully placed on her bedside table just before falling asleep. Both the photograph and the glass now lay on her bedroom floor – broken.

Chapter 3

The Los Llanios Valley, La Palma.

Day 2
2:30 a.m.

Antonio's wife, Victoria, was puzzled and annoyed by the failure of her husband to answer his phone, but she was more concerned that he had yet to return home. Before he had left for work the previous evening he had promised her faithfully that he would be back well before dawn and in good time to take her and their children to the early morning market in Funacaliente. *He wouldn't dare be late*, she thought, *especially not when the, 'wicked witch' was coming to lunch later that day.*

The person to whom Victoria was somewhat disrespectfully referring was in fact Antonio's overly fastidious mother; a woman with whom she had never seen eye to eye and especially not when it came to the freshness of food, about which her mother in law was a complete and utter obsessive. Only the freshest of the fresh would satisfy her pernickety palette; hence it was very important that she got to market early or she would never hear the end of it. Victoria's face contorted into a grotesque grimace as she attempted to mimic the expression that her mother in law would invariably adopt if she presented her with a plate of food that had anything older than a day on it. Precisely how she was able to tell an item's freshness by just looking had long been a mystery to Victoria, but tell she could and Victoria knew from past experience that any attempt to serve food older than a day would be futile, and far from well received.

'Why the hell did you marry this woman? She's useless.' her mother in law would say to Antonio, with the back of her gnarled brown hand half covering her mouth and in a whisper that was deliberately loud enough for her son, and Victoria, to hear.

'Damn woman!' Victoria muttered to herself out loud.

'And damn husband too for not picking up the phone! Where the hell are you?'

For a second time in as many minutes Victoria reached for her mobile and pressed Antonio's call icon and waited for him to pick up. The phone rang and rang and then went to voicemail. Victoria smiled momentarily when she heard the amusing message that her husband had recorded for callers, but her smile quickly disappeared when she remembered exactly why she was calling him and who was coming to lunch. For a split second Victoria considered leaving him a message, but decided against it, saying instead as she hung up,

'If he doesn't ring me, I'll kill him when he gets home!'

When, by 5:00 a.m., Antonio still hadn't come home, Victoria's feelings of annoyance with her husband completely evaporated and were replaced by those of grave concern. As she paced backwards and forwards on the veranda, repeatedly and deeply inhaling on a cigarette, thoughts about what might have happened to him raced through her mind.

Knowing that the track down the mountain from the observatory was steep, tortuous and unlit, her first thought was that he might have lost control of his car and was lying injured somewhere up on Cumbre Vieja. But she quickly managed to convince herself that this was unlikely as Antonio had driven the route many times and knew every twist and turn like the back of his hand.

'He's probably just broken down and is walking the twelve kilometres home,' she muttered to herself, and for the next half hour or so was happy with that particular scenario.

But as the first rays of the new day began to puncture the darkness of the veranda Victoria decided that she had waited long enough and she would have to call the police and find out what had happened to Antonio. However, before Victoria could make the call from her mobile, the house phone rang. As she quickly made her way to the lounge Victoria's initial thought was that it must be Antonio calling. But as her hand reached for the phone's receiver another, far more worrying possibility flashed through her mind causing her hand to hover momentarily over it before picking it up.

As the caller introduced himself and asked if this was the residence of the Torres family, Victoria instantly knew from the sombre tone of the caller's voice that what she was about to hear would make her regret, for the rest of her life, her decision not to leave Antonio a message and for saying what she had said when he had failed to answer her call some hours earlier.

'Señora, I am sorry to inform you that your husband......'

Victoria never heard what the policeman said next. The room span, her legs buckled beneath her and she slumped to the floor, still holding the receiver in her hand, but no longer capable of comprehending what the policeman was saying.

'Are you still there, señora?' said the voice on the other end of the line. 'Are you ok?'

The village clock struck six times. Somewhere in the garden a bird began singing to herald the arrival of the new day. And the cool marble tiles of the lounge floor, upon which Victoria now sat sobbing, inconsolably, vibrated briefly and then stopped.

Chapter 4

The Village of San Andres, El Heirro.

Day 2

As dawn broke over the Malpaso mountains, bathing the village of San Andres and the surrounding countryside in warm sunshine, the early morning mists rapidly melted away; just as the anxious villagers had done once the reassuring presence of the emergency services had restored calm some hours earlier, leaving the village plaza now deserted and eerily quiet.

And as the rays of sunlight seeped through the partially drawn curtains of Maria's bedroom, softly caressing her face and gently coaxing her from her slumber, she awoke to find things in her bedroom were not as she expected.

The first thing that she noticed amiss was the picture of her parents and sister, Consuela, which she found lying on the floor next to her bed. Its wooden frame was now distorted and the picture glass contained within it was cracked, almost as if someone or something had trodden on it after it had fallen or been flung from the wall. As she sat up in bed Maria was equally puzzled to see the numerous shards of glass from the broken tumbler, glinting like diamonds in the morning sunlight, scattered across the wooden boards of her bedroom floor.

'One hell of a nightmare,' she mumbled to herself. 'I must have been thrashing about a lot to have knocked the glass from the table, but how on Earth did I knock the picture off the wall?'

With this unanswered question still playing on her mind Maria got out of bed and, carefully picking a safe route through the mine-field of razor sharp glass fragments, walked from her bedroom and out onto the small balcony of her apartment.

As she stood inhaling the warm, sweet smelling air of a Canarian summer's day, she noticed that the village was uncharacteristically quiet. Normally by this time in the morning she would have expected to have seen the café owner from across the road hosing down the pavement in front of his establishment or wiping the dew of early morning from his tables and chairs. This was something that she had witnessed on countless previous mornings, but on this particular morning the elderly café owner was nowhere to be seen and, most unusually of all, his café was still closed. Likewise, the village bakery, which was directly below her apartment, would usually by now have had a long queue of people outside, waiting to collect their pan de leche for breakfast or pan basico for their evening meal. But this morning the street was empty and the delicious, sweet aroma of freshly baked bread rising up towards her apartment was also strangely absent.

Feeling confused and a little uneasy about it all Maria went back inside and started to get ready for work. Her disturbed night's sleep had caused her to wake at a later time than usual and she knew she would be late for work if she dwelt for any longer on the unusual and puzzling scenes that she had woken up to this morning. But as she sat at her dressing table, combing her long, dark, wavy hair, thoughts of the mysteriously quiet streets and fallen picture would not be banished from her mind. Once or twice she even stopped what she was doing in order to listen to what was happening outside in the village, but apart from the sound of a dog barking, all remained inexplicably quiet. Maria looked at the clock on her bedroom wall and, seeing that she was behind schedule, decided that why the picture had ended up on her bedroom floor and why the village seemed so different this morning, would have to, for the moment at least, remain annoyingly unanswered questions.

However, she would not have to wait too long before finding the answers to both questions; albeit unexpected and worrying answers, but answers, nonetheless.

Chapter 5

Granja en los Pinos, Cumbre Vieja, La Palma.

Day 2

High up on the western flank of Cumbre Vieja, the sound of Tom Baxter's alarm clock pierced the still of the early morning. An habitual early riser, Tom normally had no need for the alarm bell of the battered brass clock which stood on his bedside table. On most mornings, in fact, the dawn chorus of chattering chaffinches congregating in the pine trees which surrounded his remote mountain farm, was more than enough to waken him. But given the importance of this day, he had decided to set his alarm and his foresight on this occasion was, as it turned out, most timely.

Tom had not slept at all well that night.

The oppressive heat and humidity of the island's climate in high summer and what sounded like either rumbles of thunder or rock falls somewhere further along the ridge upon which his farm stood, had conspired to wake him up on at least three occasions during the night.

During summer months thunderstorms were not uncommon in La Palma's Caldera de Taburiente Mountains and he often lay awake at night listening to the rumble of an approaching storm and then watching forks of lightning etching their presence on the inky blackness of the sky or sheet lightning momentarily illuminating the valley below. He would also lay there waiting, and sometimes praying, to hear the pattering of raindrops on the flagstones of the finca's courtyard and hoping for the deluge that sometimes accompanies an electric storm in summer. But this was La Palma where, in the south of the island, rain never fell in summer and consequently his parched crops had to rely on an alternative source of life giving water.

Rock falls were also commonplace in the mountains surrounding his home. The whole island of La Palma is an active, but currently dormant, volcano and minor earthquakes frequently displaced rocks and sent them rolling and bouncing down the steep ridge and on to the dirt track which linked his remote home to the outside world. From time to time a particularly lively rock would make it to the bottom of the ridge and eventually come to rest on the main road which ran into the nearby town of Funacaliente. Signs at several points along this road warned motorists of the danger of rock falls. Although somewhat ironically, several of these signs had themselves been flattened by falling rocks and now lay crumpled and rusting by the roadside. According to local folklore, however, such rock falls had nothing to do with earthquakes, but were the work of evil trolls who inhabited ancient caves on the upper most parts of the ridge and who, as legend would have it, had a fondness for hurling them at passing travellers.

Be it the work of malevolent trolls or simply seismology, falling rocks were such a frequent and potentially dangerous problem that a previous owner of Tom's farm had planted a protective barrier of pine and juniper trees immediately behind it and many of these now fully grown trees bore the scars of being hit - on more than one occasion - by these 'bouncing bombs'.

Tom was unsure as to why such everyday occurrences as thunderstorms or rock falls should have disturbed his sleep so badly that night, but whatever the reason for his insomnia, for the first time since arriving on the island Tom had slept through the dawn chorus – and was still sound asleep when he was rudely awakened by the sound of his antiquated alarm clock, ringing and vibrating on his bedside table.

'Sod it!' exclaimed Tom, when he saw the time on his clock.

It was 6:00 a.m. and he needed to be at the sluice gate in just under twenty minutes. Tom rose quickly from his bed, a fraction too quickly perhaps, because the room swam violently and he was forced to momentarily grab the sides of the mattress until the spinning had stopped. *One too many brandies last night*, he thought briefly to himself. Not fully rested from his disturbed night's sleep, Tom yawned loudly, stretched, and grabbing the first items of clothing that came to hand, hurriedly pulled on a pair of shorts and faded, blue cotton shirt.

Once dressed, Tom made his way quickly, but gingerly, down the rickety wooden ladder which connected his bedroom to the living area below. The ladder, which he had cobbled together from discarded pieces of fencing found scattered around the farm, was actually one of the first things he had constructed when he and his wife, Sarah, had arrived at Granja en los Pinos in the spring of 2004. Seven years on, the ladder was still fit for purpose, although he often wondered if twenty years from now he would still be fit enough and sufficiently able bodied to climb his creaking and increasingly shaky creation.

Somewhat ironically, his first ever piece of carpentry, of which he was still immensely proud, was one of the many reasons why Sarah had decided to leave the farm and return to England. For her the precarious nightly journey to their bedroom, holding the roughly hewn wooden frame with one hand, and a dripping candle with the other, was not her idea of twenty first century living and on more than one occasion he had heard her mumbling about their 'peasant like existence' as she struggled upwards to bed.

On reaching the ground floor, the cool of the slate flagstones on the soles of his bare feet reminded Tom that he still needed to find his old and battered leather work boots.

'Where the hell are they? ' he groaned, as his eyes rapidly scanned the chaotic collection of books, empty wine bottles and tools which littered the floor of the living room. Then, in the far corner of the room, partially obscured by a discarded, week old copy of a local newspaper, he spotted the toe of one boot.

'Yes! There you are, you little sod,' exclaimed Tom, raising both arms and clenching his fists as if he had just scored the winning goal in a cup final. 'Now, where's your mate gone?'

Fortunately, as is so often the case with misplaced footwear, the second boot was located not too far from the first and Tom was soon ramming his left foot and then his right one into his badly misshapen old boots and, with laces still untied, he emerged from the gloom of the finca's interior into the blinding sun of a Canarian summer morning.

Eyes screwed tight against the glare of the sun and with his boots barely clinging to his feet, he shuffled his way across the courtyard to where a dust encrusted vehicle was parked. As he jerked open the creaking door of his jeep Tom knew that, with a bit of luck, he could still get to the sluice before it was too late - providing, of course, his jeep didn't decide to play silly buggers this morning. However, much to Tom's relief and surprise, the Great God of Ex - American Army Personnel Carriers decided to smile favourably on him that morning and for once his dilapidated jeep coughed and spluttered into life at the first attempt.

'Bugger me,' said Tom, in total amazement at his jeep's uncustomary compliance. But just to be on the safe side he revved the engine repeatedly and loudly so as to ensure that it didn't now die on him.

Tom whistled for his dog and close companion, Daisy. Tom

had found Daisy abandoned, living in his barn, malnourished and riddled with fleas when he and Sarah first took possession of the farm. To whom she had belonged previously, if anyone, was a complete mystery, but she soon demonstrated her worth by killing every rat that had also taken up residence in the vacant finca and very quickly wormed her way into both their sitting room and their hearts. Tom whistled again and called her name, but uncharacteristically the dog failed to appear. Usually the sound of the jeep's engine stuttering into life was more than sufficient signal for her to emerge from where ever she was surreptitiously gnawing on a bone, invariably pilfered from the kitchen bin, and then, run hell for leather, across the courtyard and leap spectacularly into the jeep's rear compartment. Where, like Border Collies the world over, she would contentedly sit, bright pink tongue lolling from her mouth and looking immensely pleased with herself. It didn't matter how short or how long the trip was; to be by her master's side, protecting him from evil, rock hurling trolls was all that she desired from life – along with, of course, a ready supply of easy to steal bones.

Assuming that she was still probably asleep in the barn and, on this particular morning, in too much of a hurry to wait for her, Tom decided to drive off without his constant companion and a few moments later was bumping down the bone hard and deeply rutted track which ran from his farm to the Aqueducto Primero leaving, as he drove at high speed, a billowing cloud of dust and disturbed insects in his wake.

Tom's early morning dash to the Aqueducto Primero was entirely due to the climate of his island home. Located close to the Tropic of Cancer, La Parma enjoys all year round high temperatures, but in the southern part of the island, where Tom's small farm was located, rainfall is a rare occurrence for much of the year and totally absent from May until September.

Yet in spite of La Palma's perennial heat and aridity, it is rather paradoxically known as the, 'Green Island' or 'Beautiful Island', by Palmarians, owing to its lush and verdant vegetation. Stranger still, it is also one of the most agriculturally productive islands in the Canarian Island chain with bananas, avocados, lemons and other sub - tropical crops growing there in abundance. This paradox could, in part, be explained by La Palma's very fertile volcanic soils, but also by what Tom frequently termed, 'a little miracle of nature.'

The water for his crops came not from the skies, but from the *minas gallerias* or water tunnels which carry water from the Caldera de Taburiente Mountains to all the island's farms. Precisely how the water finds its way into the minas gallerias was absolutely unique and never failed to amaze Tom.

Moisture contained within the clouds which shroud the pine clad upper slopes of the Caldera de Taburiente mountains condenses on the tree's needles and then drips to the ground where it infiltrates and eventually saturates the porous volcanic rocks of which the island is made. After many thousands of years, enough water has collected within the rocks to create a series of subterranean reservoirs known as aquifers. Water from these aquifers then seeps into the minas gallerias which have been cut into the rocks by the island's inhabitants and, under the influence of gravity, it flows downslope to the valleys below. On reaching the lower slopes, water in the minas gallerias is channelled into rock aqueducts for distribution, via sluice gates, to the many farms of the area. Each week every farmer gets a scheduled "turn" to fill an irrigation tank with water and, if a farmer's turn is at 2:00 a.m., he will make sure that he is at his sluice gate in time to open it and divert his allocation of water into a holding tank. Miss your turn, and you can basically say goodbye to your crops for that year. And today, at 6:20 a.m. precisely, it was Tom's turn to fill his tank and there was no way he was going to miss it.

Bringing his jeep to a slithering halt a few metres from the Aqueducto Primero, Tom waited for a few seconds for the dust cloud that his rapid stop had created to subside, before jumping to the ground and running quickly up the small earth embankment upon which the rock aqueduct had been constructed. He checked his watch.

'Made it!' he congratulated himself.

The time was 6:18 a.m. and in less than two minutes his weekly allocation of precious water would come gurgling and bubbling towards him.

Tom reached for the old spanner that lay on the ground close by and attached it to the rusty bolt that held the sluice gate, at a right angle, just above the aqueduct. Tensing his muscular and deeply tanned right arm, Tom began to turn the spanner and, within three revolutions of the bolt, the old wooden sluice gate was sufficiently loose to jerkily slide down into the channel, creating a barrier which would then divert the water into a sloping corrugated iron chute which ran from the aqueduct to his holding tank at the bottom of the embankment.

Preparations complete, Tom glanced at his watch again and then, with the back of his hand, wiped a rivulet of sweat from his forehead. He glanced down to where Daisy would normally be sitting with her head on his lap and her eyes looking dolefully up at him and it felt strange without her by his side. Since Sarah's departure Daisy had been the one thing left in his life that he could depend on. Tom smiled to himself as he thought how, Daisy always listened to him, never interrupted, always did what he asked without an argument and, generally speaking, was the perfect companion.

'Not a bad swap really,' he said quietly to himself, laughing slightly as he did so.

But his laughter was also tinged with a touch of sadness and, as he sat waiting for his weekly water allocation to arrive, his thoughts turned to that of his absent wife.

If he was totally honest with himself, Sarah had never fully bought into his dream of leaving the rat race of modern day living in England and starting afresh in rural Spain. Nor, initially at least, had she been fully supportive of his decision to retire early and leave his well-paid teaching job.

Never having taught herself, Sarah had no real understanding of the stresses and strains that teachers endure on a daily basis. Working as she did in the City for an international bank, Sarah believed that few people, if indeed any, could cope with the pressures that she had to face each day and therefore had little sympathy for teachers or any public sector employee for that matter. Moreover, her perception of a teacher's lot, like that of so many people working in business, was based largely on her own childhood experiences of the classroom with students sitting in rows of desks, working in total silence or passively awaiting the next instruction from their teacher; instructions which, once issued, would be carried out enthusiastically and without question. That may well have been what things were like in Sarah's fee paying private school back in the 70s, but it bore scant resemblance to the daily happenings in his school, or for that matter, any state funded comprehensive school.

And then, of course, there was the perennial misconception about the long holidays and short working days that all teachers enjoyed; whilst the rest of Britain slaved away from nine till five each day for fifty weeks a year. Sarah had often said to Tom how she would give her right arm to start work at 9:00 a.m. and finish by 3:00 p.m. each day and never once stopped to consider the amount of time, before and after school, that he spent preparing lessons and marking books. Or, how nearly every one of his school holidays was devoted to writing reports or preparing for yet another change to the curriculum which had been dreamt up by the latest minister of education; ministers who, in Tom's opinion, usually cared more about furthering their own political career than actually advancing the academic achievements of school children.

Sarah's inability to understand the lot of a teacher in today's government inspired 'academies' was a constant source of annoyance to Tom, and he felt frustrated and let down by her unwillingness to share his vision of a better life for them both in rural Spain. But whilst initially unsupportive of his retirement plans, Sarah had eventually come round to his way of thinking, although it did take a completely unforeseen event to precipitate her change of heart.

Not long after Tom had retired from teaching an 'Insider Trading Scandal' rocked the bank where Sarah worked and in the ensuing cull of employees, she was made redundant. With time now on her hands and still feeling extremely bitter about how she had been treated by her employers, Sarah suddenly began to warm to the idea of them both retiring early and starting a new, less complicated life in sunny Spain. A place where, she had begun to muse to herself, she could be the archetypal farmer's wife, collecting new laid eggs from their flock of chickens which would follow her obediently around the courtyard; somewhere that she could pick a fresh lemon for her gin and tonic from a tree in their orchard and then spend the afternoon on a sun lounger reading a novel. Yes, she had eventually convinced herself, life in rural Spain may well be to her liking after all.

Unfortunately, and completely unbeknown to Sarah, Tom's pension and her mediocre redundancy package could never have given them the relaxed and laid back lifestyle that she envisaged. And the reality of just how hard life can be on a mountain farm in Spain soon became apparent not long after they had arrived at their new home some seven years ago.

A rumble of what sounded like a distant thunderstorm somewhere in the north of the island, suddenly brought Tom back to the here and now. Tom felt a slight vibration in the rock aqueduct upon which he was sitting and he looked back along the channel in anticipation of the arrival of his water. The vibration in the aqueduct continued with slightly increasing intensity, but strangely no water appeared. Tom checked his watch again. The time showed 6:27 a.m.

Very few things on La Palma ran to time; buses were always late, shops never opened on time and usually closed well before the time stated on the shop door and local people generally had scant regard for schedules and deadlines – such is life on a sub-tropical island. But when it came to water supply that was a totally different thing entirely. Being in such short supply, not to mention expensive and, for those in control of it, very profitable, the island's water authority ran a very tight ship indeed. Whatever the time of day or night your allocation was scheduled for, invariably it would arrive punctually and in the exact amount requested.

Tom checked the time again. In the glare of the morning sun it was not easy to see the hands of his watch as the glass face had become scratched and slightly opaque over the years, but he could just about make out that it was now 6:35 a.m. – and still no water. Tom felt another slight movement in the stone wall of the aqueduct. *Was it really moving?* he thought. *Or, having had no breakfast and drunk too much the night before, was he simply imagining it?*

Tom couldn't be certain either way but more important than the disorientating effects of an empty stomach or hang-over was the non-appearance of his water. Tom reached for his mobile phone and then, remembering that the battery was flat, decided that he would have to, as a last resort, make the perilous trip to the nearby town of Funacaliente and find out what had happened to his precious water.

There were a number of reasons why Tom was not particularly looking forward to a drive into town. Notwithstanding the danger posed from rock hurling, malevolent trolls, a journey down the track which linked his farm to the main road into Funacaliente was not one that any sane person would relish, and to say that the "helter-skelter", as locals euphemistically referred to it, was challenging, would be a gross understatement.

Steeply sloping, boulder strewn, tortuously twisting, unfenced for much of its length and with more ruts and pot holes than a First World War battlefield, the track was just about driveable with caution during the dry summer months and positively treacherous after a rare rainfall event in winter. The "helter-skelter" was certainly not for the faint hearted or the inexperienced and the one or two tourists who had inadvertently happened upon it, and then been foolish enough to try it, ended up wishing they hadn't. In consequence Tom, along with the other farmers along the ridge, normally treated the road with the utmost respect and used it only when they had to.

But Tom was not in a particularly cautious or respectful state of mind this morning and decision made, he jumped back into his jeep, barely noticing the pain in his lower back caused by seven years of driving at high speed in his jeep along the deeply rutted track. His mind was now firmly focused on a far larger problem than that posed by a couple of worn vertebrae - because without his water, his crops would wither in the heat of the Canarian summer and his sole income for the coming year would be lost.

Tom turned the ignition key and for the second time that day was astonished to hear the engine cough, splutter and then roar into life.

'Praise the Lord!' exclaimed Tom, throwing both arms up in the air and turning his face towards the cloudless Canarian morning sky. And with salutations to the almighty complete, he set off down the track, dodging boulders and pot holes as he went, and driving as fast as his aged jeep would allow.

Chapter 6

Puerto de la Brava, Tenerife.

Day 2

At the hotel Playa de la Americas, Consuela Gonzales was performing her morning routine very much as normal. She had got up at 6:00 a.m., showered, donned her white towelling dressing gown and was now sitting at her dressing table, adding some finishing touches to her make-up. As Head Receptionist at the hotel, hers was the face that guests would see first on their arrival and it was therefore important that she always looked her very best. Not that this was an especially difficult task for her to accomplish as her tanned complexion, deep brown eyes, high cheek bones and long, dark, wavy hair made her stand out from many of her colleagues – with, or without the aid of make-up. Indeed, apart from the small cluster of scars beneath her right eye, her face was just about perfect and it was to this one and only facial imperfection that she always paid most attention when preparing for the day ahead.

How she had acquired her facial scarring was something that she had only shared with one other person since arriving on the island nearly six months ago and that was her best friend at the hotel, Adrienne. As far as everyone else in her new life was concerned, including her new boyfriend, the marks on her face were simply the result of catching chicken pox as a child and nobody ever suspected otherwise.

But her facial scarring had a much more sinister history than a simple childhood illness. Years of brutality and subjugation at the hands of a vicious and vindictive man who, although now many miles from her, was still close enough, mentally and physically, to hold her in a constant state of fear and anxiety; that was the real reason behind her facial scarring, together with those on the rest of her body.

Consuela's other scars were far easier to conceal and certainly did not require several layers of make-up. The scars left by cigarette butts being repeatedly stubbed out on her torso were easily hidden by her normal clothing and, even when sunbathing by the hotel's pool, she could cover them by wearing a bathing costume rather than a bikini. But the easiest scars of all to hide, but not necessarily the easiest ones to bear, were the mental ones that she had acquired during her marriage to her violent and possessive husband. Not even Adrienne knew how deep seated and painful these scars were and she had no idea how Consuela would wake each morning, sweating and shaking from yet another nightmare about her husband.

Consuela had met her husband, Franco, whilst dining out with friends at his restaurant just over three years ago and for the first year of their relationship he had seemed perfectly normal and gave no indication as to what he was truly like or what he was capable of. He was, however, always quite guarded about his past and whenever she broached the matter he would swiftly change the subject or make some excuse about his past being too boring to discuss. Little by little she did tease some information out of him, but apart from him being born in Barcelona, an only child, a waiter by profession, now a successful restauranteur and both his parents being deceased, she never really got to know much else about him.

But it was hardly surprising that Franco was so reticent when it came to his past. The illegitimate son of a prostitute he had spent much of his younger life fending for himself on the streets of Barcelona, especially at nights, when his mother most frequently entertained her clients and at which time he would be given some pesetas and told to make himself scarce until morning. As for his father, he couldn't remember much about him, although he did have one or two vague, misty memories of his mother giving money to a man who would hit her if he wasn't happy with the amount she was handing over.

Franco's career as a petty criminal had begun early and by the age of eight he was a fully-fledged member of a gang of street urchins who preyed on tourists in and around the city's main tourist attractions. From pick pocketing and begging he had graduated to more serious crimes such as burglary and assault and it was at this point in his life that he had lost contact with his mother who, he later heard, had died from a severe beating or possibly a drug overdose, but probably both. Either way, he felt no sadness at her passing as she had never been a part of his life and he had never felt any love for her anyway and it was perhaps this lack of maternal bonding which had helped to shape the misogynistic man that he had become by the time he had reached his early twenties. As far as he was concerned, women had their uses, both within and outside of the bedroom, but they also needed to know their place and there was only one way to deal with any female who forgot where that place was and that way was with his fists or any object which was within easy reach. Given his attitude towards women, it was not surprising that, like his father, he too had pimped a number of girls for a while on the mainland, but the decriminalisation of prostitution in Spain in 1995, coupled with the AIDS scare of the same time, had been bad for business and he had eventually found a more lucrative profession as a self-employed male escort. This line of work came relatively easily to Franco whose good looks and ability to charm the fairer sex had proved so useful when recruiting girls for his earlier business ventures. But by his early thirties Franco had bored of life as a gigolo and was sufficiently solvent to move to La Palma and buy a small restaurant, which had steadily grown in reputation and profitability.

Although Consuela had initially found his reluctance to talk about himself quite strange, he was, to all intents and purposes, simply a successful local businessman whose history became increasingly unimportant as their relationship blossomed. And she soon found herself falling deeply in love with this rather mysterious, but nonetheless good looking and seemingly charming man.

Her sister, Maria, however, along with both of her parents, were not so accepting of Franco's unwillingness to talk about his past. Consuela's father was so suspicious about Franco that he even secretly employed a Private Detective to find out more about the man whom their daughter was soon to marry. Unfortunately, his enquiries drew a blank and it was with a degree of trepidation that Consuela's father reluctantly agreed to giving Franco his daughter's hand in marriage. But once they had announced their decision to get married and she began wearing his engagement ring, small changes in his behaviour began to appear.

At first Consuela thought that his constant telephone calls and text messages to her whilst at work or out with friends was just a sign that he cared about her and was worried for her safety. But gradually she began to feel that her life was no longer her own and that Franco was trying to monitor and control her every movement. However, the real extent of his possessive and violent personality didn't really emerge until after they were married and living close to her parents in Santa Cruz and it was at this point that the beatings began and his predilection for equally violent sexual acts emerged. He was, of course, always sorry after he had punched and kicked her as she crouched in the corner of their bedroom or had nearly strangled her and repeatedly promised that it would never happen again. But just like he had failed in his promise to love, honour and obey, Franco never stopped beating or sexually abusing her and continued to do so until one night, his cruelty towards her reached a new height; it was the night that Franco violently raped her for the first time.

As Consuela looked at herself in the mirror of her dressing table, her face momentarily contorted into a grimace as she recalled the pain and humiliation that she had endured on that occasion at the hands of her brutal and sadistic husband. Her ordeal that night was, however, thankfully a short lived one, as within a minute or so of animalistic grunting and thrusting, Franco had rolled from her prostrate body and fallen quickly into a drunken sleep. But on subsequent nights, of which there were unfortunately many, Franco's sexual attacks on her were more prolonged and gradually became increasingly violent and continued right up until the night that she had fled from her depraved and brutal husband.

On that particular night, after smashing a beer bottle on her head, he had thrown her down a flight of stairs when she had refused to submit to his demands for sex and she had been hospitalised with a badly fractured arm and lacerations to her face. This latest act of brutality proved to be the final straw for Consuela and in desperation she managed to summon up enough courage to flee from him. Discharging herself from hospital, she had taken a taxi to the airport and caught the first flight available. She didn't care about the excruciating pain that she was in or even where she was going; she just had to get as far away from Franco as quickly as possible and as far as her limited finances would permit. At first nobody knew where she had fled to, but when she did eventually make contact, it was with her sister, Maria, who, along with the rest of the Gonzales family, were sworn to secrecy about Consuela's whereabouts.

As Consuela applied a final layer of concealer and turned her head from side to side to check in the mirror if the finished result was to her liking, she noticed, out of the corner of one eye that a white envelope had been pushed under the door of her hotel room. Reaching down, she picked up the envelope and turned it over, but as she did so, her hand began to tremble uncontrollably. The handwriting on the envelope was instantly recognisable as that of her husband, Franco. As she stared at the letter in her now violently shaking hand, she could feel her heart thumping in her chest and found it difficult to catch her breath.

'Oh my God,' she murmured. 'He's found me.'

Question after question began to race through her mind. *Was he on the island, and if so, was he in the hotel? Did he push it under my door or did he pay a hotel porter to deliver it?* But the question which worried her most of all was, *How did he find me and what will he do to me this time?*

As she held the letter in her trembling hands, she initially contemplated tearing it into pieces and throwing it into the waste paper bin which stood in the corner of the room. But even though Consuela thought that she could anticipate exactly what it would say, for some irrational and inexplicable reason she found herself unable to do so. Instead, she placed it hurriedly on her dressing table and, with thoughts about Franco's whereabouts still rushing through her mind, began to dress for work.

A knock on her bedroom door made her freeze. Her first thought was that Franco was outside, but the gentility of the knock suggested otherwise.

'Yes, who's there?' she called out, her voice quavering ever so slightly.

'It's me, Adrienne, are you ready for work yet?'

At the sound of her friend's voice her body instantly relaxed.

'Yes, just coming,' she called out, and made her way across the room and opened the locked door.

'My God, you look as white as a sheet,' said Adrienne. 'Have you just seen a ghost?'

'Not quite, but I have had a letter from Franco. It was pushed under my door last night.' said Consuela, pointing at the letter propped up against the small table lamp on her dressing table.

Adrienne was perfectly aware of the circumstances surrounding Consuela's flight from La Palma and knew what Franco was capable of too.

'Oh my God!' 'Is he staying here, in the hotel?'

'I don't know, but he's on the island for sure and God knows what he'll do next.'

'What did the letter say?'

'I don't know, I haven't read it, but I'm sure it's full of the usual apologies and promises, none of which he'll ever keep.'

Adrienne looked at the unopened letter.

'I think that, for your own safety, you need to contact the police because, from what you've told me about him, he sounds capable of anything.'

'I will, just as soon as I finish work.'

When she arrived at the hotel's reception, the Head Porter was just finishing his night shift.

'Did you get your letter?' he asked.

'So it was you!' said Consuela, a feeling of relief momentarily washing over her at discovering that it wasn't Franco who had been outside her door. But this feeing quickly evaporated when he said,

'Si, a man in the hotel bar gave it me in the early hours of this morning and asked me if I could deliver it for him.'

Consuela looked across to where the entrance to the hotel bar was located and in a faltering voice asked,

'Is he still in there?'

'No, he left some time ago, but he told me to tell you that he would be back.'

'Back when?'

'He didn't say, just that he'd be back.'

'What did he look like?'

But the man that he described was nothing like her husband Franco. For one thing Franco was not short and stocky, but tall and wiry. Nor was Franco a smoker whereas the man that the Head Porter was describing had the characteristically rasping tones of a heavy smoker. Consuela was puzzled but at the same relieved by the description. Clearly, it wasn't Franco who had delivered the letter to the hotel so there was a chance that he wasn't on the island after all, but a number of burning questions remained fixed in her mind including, most importantly, who was the messenger and why was he delivering a letter on Franco's behalf?

Consuela contemplated this question for a few minutes before deciding that she would have to return to her room and read the letter if she was to have any idea about what was going on. But just as she was about to set off, a party of guests arrived in the hotel's reception forcing Consuela to delay her return.

As the new arrivals checked in, Consuela was so focused on her duties that she was completely unaware of the swarthy skinned man sitting in a car opposite the hotel's entrance, holding a lit cigarette in one hand and a camera phone in the other. He sat there watching her every move for several minutes, before tossing his cigarette out of the car window and slowly driving off.

However, even if she had seen him she would not have been aware that not only was this the man who had given the letter to the Head Porter, but he was also the very same person that her parents had employed to find out about Franco's history over three years ago. Nor could she have known that this man was now in the employment of Franco and that the reason for him being on the island involved much more than the simple delivery of a letter.

Soon the paths of both the man and Consuela were to cross. But not in a way that either could have ever envisaged and it was destined to be a meeting which would cost one of them their life, whilst helping to save the life of the other.

Chapter 7

El Heirro.

Day 2

As Maria's fingers drummed the steering wheel of her Fiat 500 in time to the music on the car's radio, she sighed deeply. She was late for work and this hold up was making her later still. Ordinarily, her short journey to work was an uneventful one, with little or nothing to interrupt her thoughts, which today were focused on trying to remember the bizarre dream that she had last night and why the village had been so uncharacteristically quiet this morning.

As a scientist, such vivid dreams both fascinated and frustrated Maria. On the one hand, she was always amazed how the human brain could store a single, completely inconsequential event from the preceding day and then somehow develop it into an interrelated set of events to form a dream. But equally she found her inability to understand or control when or how such dreams occurred exasperating. Although Maria rarely had a particularly memorable dream, when she did have one she always tried to remember what had happened the day before to initiate it and, having been stationary behind a battered farm truck for over thirty minutes, this morning's commute to work was proving to be an ideal opportunity for some dream analysis - although by now she had neither isolated the trigger for last night's strange dream –

nor the reason for this morning's hold up.

Even in the height of the tourist season, traffic jams on El Heirro's winding and narrow roads were virtually unheard of. Tourism on the island was thankfully still in its embryonic phase and recent volcanic activity on the island had done little to boost its reputation as a sub-tropical paradise, where, according to the holiday brochures, the all year round sunshine and gentle pace of life were ideal for relaxation and recuperation.

Whilst the recent eruption had kept many tourists away from the island, it had actually been influential in Maria coming there. Since graduating in Geophysics from the University of Madrid three years earlier, Maria had long been fascinated by El Heirro's violent and turbulent volcanic history and was eager to study it first-hand. So when an opportunity to work with the world renowned Professor of Volcanology, Felipe de Costa at El Heirro's, Instituto Geografico Nacional had come about, she had jumped at the chance – even though his reputation had deterred many of her fellow graduates from applying for the post. It was a decision that, so far at least, she had not regretted and generally speaking she looked forward to her daily commute to the Institute and the work that was waiting for her when she arrived there.

Perplexed by what could possibly be causing the hold up this morning Maria decided to leave her car and wander along the queue of stationary vehicles to investigate further. Up-ahead, a JCB was slowly pushing one of several large boulders which lay in the middle of the road towards the roadside. Next to it stood a group of day glow jacketed workmen who, in keeping with workmen the world over, were leaning on their shovels, smoking and laughing. As she neared them, a younger workman turned towards Maria and with his hand held aloft, gestured for her to stop.

'It's not safe to get any closer señorita,' he shouted, in a thick accent which was typical of the island. 'There may be more rock falls at any second.'

As he spoke, the young workman's jacket flapped gently in the early morning breeze, intermittingly exposing his tanned and muscular torso and Maria found her eyes instantly and irresistibly drawn towards it.

The young man's broad grin alerted her to the fact that he had noticed where her eyes were focused and in order to hide her embarrassment, she quickly turned her head to look up the steep slope which bordered the road. *Yes,* she thought, *there were plenty of rocks perched precariously on the slope and it was possible that the vibrations of the JCB could displace one or more of them at any moment.*

'OK, thank you for the warning,' she said, trying desperately not to catch his eye as she suspected he was now grinning more broadly than ever.

'No problem,' he replied. 'Anything else I can do for you this morning, señorita?'

Maria chose to ignore his innuendo rich offer of further assistance and, turning to face the line of stationary vehicles, began walking back towards her car, with the raucous laughter of the group of workmen ringing loudly in her ears.

'It was last night's quake,' said a man's voice from one of the stationary cars as she retraced her steps.

Maria paused and turned towards where the voice had come from.

'It was a big one,' he continued, 'they're saying on the radio that it was perhaps 4.5 on the Richter scale.'

As a geologist, Maria knew that a magnitude 4.5 quake could never be legitimately described as a 'big one', but by El Heirro's standards a quake of that size was an unusually large seismic event and she was instantly intrigued by it.

'Anyone hurt?' she enquired.

'They didn't say,' said the man, shrugging his shoulders.

'But apparently there's been some damage to several buildings in Restinga.'

After thanking the man for the information, Maria continued to walk back towards her car, but after a few paces paused momentarily as a possible explanation for the fallen picture and broken glass began to form in her mind and simultaneously she began to question if her strange dream was not so bizarre after all. *Perhaps,* she began to think, *the shaking and rattling train in her dream had actually been her bed shaking and rattling because of the quake and it was that which had woken her so abruptly during the night. A magnitude 4.5 quake,* she mused, *could also certainly cause a picture to shake itself free from its fixing on a wall or a glass to fall from a bedside table. It could also explain why the village had been so quiet this morning; people were obviously worried about another quake and had either fled the area or were staying indoors.*

Still pondering these possibilities, Maria climbed back into her car, turned up the radio and waited for the JCB to clear the landslide from the road. She glanced at her watch again.

'Oh dear,' she said to herself, 'the professor is not going to be a happy bunny at all when, and if, I ever get to work.' Reaching for her mobile she tried to call him, but the lack of signal bars indicated that she was in one of the island's numerous communication black spots. Maria cursed, 'Shit!' 'That's all I need.'

Deciding to check her text messages instead she scrolled through them and discovered that she had one from her sister, Consuela. Now safe and settled in Tenerife, she regularly texted Maria asking her to come and spend some time with her, but Maria's busy work schedule and demanding boss had thus far prevented her from doing so. This message from Consuela was not, however, the usual invitation and its content caused Maria's brow to furrow with concern as she read it. How Franco had managed to track her sister down to Tenerife was a complete mystery to Maria and she made a mental note to phone Consuela as soon as she got into work – providing, of course, that she eventually got there.

Chapter 8

La Palma

Day 2

How Tom had managed to make it to the valley floor alive and
unscathed was little short of a miracle. Equally miraculous was the
fact that his ancient jeep had also managed to make it to this point
in one piece.

For some reason the road had been considerably more boulder
strewn than usual and during the descent he had noticed, albeit
fleetingly, but on several occasions, an unfamiliar smell. The
smell had been so strong in one place that it had caused him to
momentarily lose concentration and he had almost lost control
of the jeep. He couldn't quite place what it reminded him of;
perhaps swimming pools, perhaps sewage, even maybe, somewhat
strangely, rotten eggs. Try as he might he just couldn't put his
finger on it, but it certainly wasn't the pleasantly aromatic smell
of pine trees in summer that is so characteristic of the La Palma's
mountains. But most bizarrely of all he had noticed during his
hair raising descent that a patch of pine trees on the left hand
side of the road and approximately halfway up the ridge, was a
completely different colour to those around them. They seemed
more brown than green, almost as if they were diseased or dying.
What's more, the trees were no longer growing upslope at an
acute angle, but were now either perpendicular to the sloping

ridge or leaning at a slight obtuse angle downslope.

Puzzled, and with time on his hands, Tom decided to investigate further. He braked hard, bringing his jeep to a bone juddering halt on the unmade surface of the track. As the maelstrom of dust that his rapid stop had created began to clear, Tom climbed out of his jeep and stood perfectly still by the edge of the track, listening intently and staring at the scene around him.

All was quiet that morning, too quiet in fact. There was no bird song which was highly unusual for one thing. And then, most strangely of all, there was no sound from the Cicadas. Although still early in the morning, by now they would normally be in full voice, chirruping away in their tens of thousands and filling the morning air with their unmistakeable noise.

Tom drew in a lungful of the early morning mountain air.

'Got it.' he announced out loud after several minutes of deep inhalation. 'It's sulphur!' 'Yes, definitely sulphur.'

He looked up to where he had noticed the discoloured trees and surveyed the ground immediately beneath them. Seeing nothing out of the ordinary but still feeling that something was not quite right, Tom began scrambling up the steep slope towards the trees and as he drew closer he noticed that the pine needles on several of the lower branches were withered and brown. The smell of sulphur was also noticeably much stronger now, so strong in fact that he had to clasp his hand across his mouth and nose because he could feel his nostrils beginning to burn and could even taste the sulphur in the back of his throat. Tom's eyes continued to scan the ground beneath the trees, looking for a clue as to where the acrid smell was issuing from, but when his eyes then began to water and burn he decided that it was time to return to his jeep.

Still racking his brain for some kind of explanation for what he had seen and smelt, Tom restarted his jeep and driving more slowly now, continued down the track until he eventually reached the flat and relatively benign main road into Funacaliente. Feeling sufficiently in control of the jeep to take one hand off the steering wheel, Tom checked his watch.

'Good, no need to worry,' he said to himself. 'I've got plenty of time to get to town and sort things out.'

Tom eased his foot off the accelerator and drove on to Funacaliente, where, he was soon to discover, there was, in fact, a great deal to worry about and the failure of his water to arrive that morning was just the beginning of his problems.

Chapter 9

The Villa Gaia, Los Llanios Valley, La Palma

Day 2

Franco Hernandez closed his eyes and moaned as the nimble fingers of the beautiful blonde masseuse began to work their magic on the taut muscles of his upper back. 'Mmmm, that feels so good.' he said out loud and began to think about what he would soon be doing to the masseuse. *His day would soon be complete*, he thought to himself.

Franco felt particularly pleased with himself that morning for a number of reasons. Not just because of what he had planned for the masseuse, but more importantly, because by now his estranged wife, Consuela, would have received his letter demanding a fast track 'Separcion de Bienes' divorce which, under Spanish Law, would allow him to retain ownership of all the assets that he had held before marrying Consuela and not have to divide them equally with her. Then he would be free to marry the woman who would ultimately give him the lifestyle that he had so long dreamt of. There was, of course, the potential problem of Consuela's non-compliance, but he felt sure that his new business partner would effect a satisfactory outcome should that unlikely problem arise. Besides, after how he had treated her throughout their marriage he could see no possible reason why she shouldn't jump at the chance of getting him out of her life, even if it meant losing her share of his business ventures.

With Consuela on another island and many miles away, bigamy would, of course, have been the more straight forward option. But Consuela's family were quite influential on La Palma and having already made his life extremely difficult since his separation from their daughter six months ago, they would have relished the opportunity to further blacken his name.

'No,' he muttered under his breath, 'if my plan is going to work, things will have to be done properly and seemingly, at least, all above board. That may well take slightly longer than I want, but it will be a small sacrifice to make in order to achieve my overall objective.'

Franco opened one of his eyes to survey the sumptuous surrounding that would soon be his. The twelve bedroom villa with its pool, next to which he was currently lying, the landscaped gardens over-looking the deep blue waters of the Atlantic and the collection of high performance sports cars in the villa's garages would all soon be his - along with a considerable portfolio of stocks and shares.

Yes, he mused, *pretty soon he would be a very wealthy man in his own right and not as he was now, the sexual play thing of a wealthy widow with no legal right of access to any of her money or property.*

Apart from Consuela refusing his demands, the only other possible cloud on the horizon that he could see would be the nights that he would still have to spend in bed with his passport to a better, richer life – the widow Christina de Souza. The former wife of one of the island's richest business men, the widow de Souza had never been blessed with particularly good looks, and as she had grown older, what looks that she had possessed had rapidly deserted her. That is not to say that Franco had never had sex with an unattractive women before. Far from it, in fact. His restaurant had been purchased largely from sleeping with rich and often unattractive women and if he could do it then he was damn sure that he could do it again, for a short while longer at least.

He tried to dispel the pictures of Christina that had begun to form in his mind, knowing full well that such thoughts would do nothing to enhance his sexual performance. But try as he might, images of her sagging flat breasts, the wrinkled skin of her buttocks and her thin, mean lips surrounding teeth stained yellow by a life time of smoking filterless cigarettes, would not be banished from his mind.

Annoyed by this unwanted mental intrusion and its effect on his libido, he barked at the masseuse to stop what she was doing and sitting, bolt upright, reached for the glass of vermouth that stood on the small glass table next to the sun lounger upon which he had been lying.

'What's the matter, Señor Franco?' said the masseuse, with a worried tone in her voice. 'Have I done something to annoy you?'

'No,' he snapped. 'Just get the fuck out of here. I need time to think. Go indoors now and put some fucking clothes on.'

Startled by the rapid change in his mood, the blonde masseuse picked up her bag containing bottles of essential oils and quickly retreated to the interior of the villa.

'Fucking women,' snarled Franco, who was more annoyed at the sudden loss of his sexual appetite than at the fairer sex per se, but, as always at times of stress, he naturally found them a useful and ready scapegoat. Franco replaced his drink on the poolside table and lay back down. He closed his eyes against the glare of the morning sun and tried desperately to banish the mental images of Christina that were persistently floating in and out of his thoughts. When that didn't work, he tried to think how Consuela would react when she realised that he had found where she was hiding. This time the image of a terrified and weeping Consuela was sufficiently strong to repel all other thoughts from his mind and a shark like grin returned to Franco's face.

He had, in fact, known of her whereabouts for a considerable period of time, thanks to the efforts of a certain Private Detective called Jose Batista, but had chosen not to reveal this until his entrapment of Christina had been completed to his satisfaction.

'Funny isn't it,' he muttered quietly to himself, 'how money can manipulate a situation to one's advantage. One minute Batista is in the employ of the Gonzales family, with instructions to find incriminating evidence about him, and then, following an offer from Franco that Batista just couldn't refuse, he's agreeing to bury everything that he's found out about him and is now working for Franco with instructions to find the Gonzales' daughter.' *Money talks*, he thought, and then hissed, through clenched teeth, 'Money is power and soon I will have all the money and power that I want, thanks to Christina and, of course, my new-found business associate.'

Chapter 10

Instituto Geografica Nacional, Frontera, El Heirro

Day 2

At the Instituto Geografico Nacional, Professor Felipe de Costa sat at his desk, staring intently at the screen of his computer. He hit the tab marked 'recent seismic events' and examined the image that appeared before him. Superimposed onto a map of El Heirro and in a roughly diagonal line running from north to south, were a number of white, yellow and orange dots of varying sizes. The dots began a few miles south of the island in the vicinity of a small fishing village called Restinga, then continued in a north westerly direction, roughly bisecting the island, and then petered out just off the north coast.

The twenty or so dots indicated the preceding day's seismic activity and, as such, there was nothing out of the ordinary in what he was seeing. Since the formation of a small volcano on the sea bed three miles south of Restinga just under two years ago, minor seismic activity had been a fairly constant occurrence on the island, with an occasional earthquake swarm of several hundred minor tremors occurring every few months or so. At one point, the number of tremors had actually reached four thousand in one day and it was feared that another, much bigger eruption off the south coast was imminent. But the fears proved unfounded as this unprecedented level of seismic activity soon died down to its normal daily level.

As the professor's eyes followed the line of coloured dots he noted three red ones located in the centre of the island. These dots indicated much larger quakes and intrigued, he quickly moved the cursor over the first of them. The information tab which suddenly appeared next to this dot caused him to take a sharp intake of breath and he felt his heart rate begin to quicken.

'Magnitude 5.1 was most unusual,' he murmured quietly to himself.

The second and third dots revealed similar sized quakes. These quakes were by far the biggest that he could recall since beginning work at the Institute some thirteen years earlier and perhaps indicated that magma below the island was once again rising. And in his experience, rising magma usually meant only one thing - an eruption could be brewing.

Concerned by what he had seen, the professor reached for his office phone and dialled Maria's internal number and waited for her to pick-up. When her answer machine clicked into action, he angrily slammed the phone down and reached for his mobile phone.

'Where the hell is she?' he muttered under his breath and then more loudly, 'She should be at work by now!'

Patience and tolerance, especially of other people's frailties and problems, had never been the professor's strongest suit. He believed that if he could get to work early each day, then every other employee at the institute should be able to. Domestic situations, relationship problems and ill health were, in his view, secondary to the more important business of volcanology and the former should never interfere with the latter.

His devotion to volcanology, coupled with his less than sensitive disposition towards others, probably explained why he had never married and why the few women who had tried to change him had, sooner or later, given up on the challenge. In the professor's own words "he was married to science and that would always be his one and only true love."

In consequence, the professor was not a particularly easy man to work with, or for, and when Maria arrived at the Institute from Madrid University in the summer of 2011 she had struggled to form a bond with him. Arrogant, rude, obsessive but, at the same time, utterly brilliant, were words that she had often used to describe him to friends when they had asked how her new job was going. In time, however, she had warmed to him and became quite skilful at reading the mood that he was in on any given day and adjusted her behaviour accordingly. Moreover, she soon discovered that he did have a softer and more reasonable side to his personality providing, of course, everything was going his way. And on the days when his humour and considerate character shone through she found herself actually enjoying his company.

Once, just the once, she had actually found herself becoming physically drawn to him. In his early fifties, with a shock of grey, wavy hair and stocky but powerful build, the professor was not an unattractive older man. Maria was particularly attracted by his dark brown eyes which seemed to mischievously sparkle on the rare occasion he actually relaxed and smiled at her. She recalled how, on one isolated occasion, the proximity of his body to hers when they had been seated next to one another during a conference had actually caused her pulse to increase, only slightly it must be stressed, but increase nevertheless.

Fortunately, the professor's infamous and frequent mood swings quickly and irrevocably squashed any further feelings of this nature and their relationship, she concluded, should and would always be purely professional, but his rugged good looks and intellectual powers were, infuriatingly, rather attractive nonetheless.

With the image of the three red dots still visible out of the corner of his eye, the professor's annoyance with Maria quickly turned to that of concern when he realised that one of the dots was very close to the village of San Andres where Maria lived. The professor scrolled down the list of contacts on his mobile phone and, on finding Maria's home number, pressed the call icon and waited for her to pick up. Once again, he found himself listening to a 'not available message', but this time he was told that his call was being redirected to Maria's mobile phone. He waited patiently for the connection to establish itself, but his hopes of ascertaining whether or not she was safe were similarly dashed as her mobile phone went straight to voicemail. *She's probably driving and unable to pick up,* he reasoned to himself. *Or,* he then thought, *she could be in one of the island's many black spots where mobile signals were notoriously bad.*

Being so mountainous, such black spots were infuriatingly numerous on El Heirro and Maria had often joked that mirrors would be a better way of communicating with each other whilst in the field. *In any event,* thought the professor, *Maria knew what to do if a quake struck,* and he momentarily imagined her diving under a table or bracing herself in a doorway, which is the strongest part of a house, during a quake. Slightly reassured, but with a rising feeling of frustration nonetheless, he moved the cursor to close the web page and in a second his computer screen was blank and the small cluster of yellow dots in the ocean just south of the neighbouring island of La Palma and the purple dot, indicating a magnitude 6.8 quake close to La Palma's infamous volcanic ridge, the Cumbre Vieja, went, for the moment at least, completely unnoticed by the normally methodical professor.

Chapter 11

Funacaliente, La Palma

Day 2

As he drove through the streets of Funacaliente, Tom was struck by how quiet and congestion free the town was that morning. Today was market day and normally by now the town's plaza and the streets surrounding it would be a hive of activity. Market traders would be busily erecting their colourful stalls and, like artists preparing for an important exhibition, arranging their fruit and vegetables upon trestle tables with the utmost care and attention. Locals, usually the more elderly ones, hellbent on grabbing the best produce before anyone else could, would be circling like hungry sharks around each stall, ready to strike as soon as the market trader signalled that he was open for business. The warm morning air would be thick with the smell of fresh fruit mingling with the aroma of huge steaming dishes of paella being cooked in readiness for the afternoon siesta and the voices of farmers playfully making less than complimentary comments about the quality and size of each other's produce would ring out above the growing hubbub of expectant and excited shoppers.

It never failed to amaze Tom just how obsessive the Palmarians were about the freshness and size of their fruit and vegetables. Coming as he did from a country where food came mainly in sealed and sterilised plastic packets and the 'Best before date' was the shoppers' only guide to the freshness of the product, Tom had experienced a major culture shock when he had first tried to sell his farm's produce at the local market. And a run in with some of the town's more elderly denizens had taught him a salutary lesson about selling fruit and vegetables in a Spanish market.

The modus operandi of the Mamas Mafia, as he rather disrespectfully referred to the town's more senior female citizens, was more akin to an investigation by a police forensic scientist than an everyday shopping trip. Individual pieces of fruit were randomly selected, smelt, squeezed, held up to the light, smelt again and generally scrutinised from every possible angle. Any imperfections, however small or insignificant, once spotted were accompanied by an audible tut-tut, which became increasingly louder as each new piece of produce was inspected. The offending pieces of fruit would then be passed to other, nearby elderly shoppers for them to inspect and eventually, after more tut-tutting and grimacing, the fruit would be tossed unceremoniously back onto the stall and the Mamas Mafia would shuffle off, like a group of old black crows, to the next stall.

Tom remembered how one, probably high ranking member of the excessively fastidious Mamas Mafia, had asked him once why he was wasting everybody's time bringing such inferior lemons to market. Stung by the bluntness of her unwarranted criticism, Tom had foolishly tried to defend the quality of his produce. But this proved to be a big mistake as his stall was shunned by every shopper over the age of sixty five for several weeks thereafter and he was convinced that his disgruntled elderly customer had voiced her less than favourable opinion about his lemons to anybody in the market who would listen. Eventually, faced with impending financial ruin on the one hand and a wife who had begun to tire of his jokes about having had an 'unfruitful day' at the market on

the other, Tom was forced to seek some advice from Alonso, who
ran the stall next to his. It came as a great relief to Tom when
Alonso informed him that there was actually nothing wrong with
his produce. But Alonso had also told him that if he wanted to
survive in the market he would have to learn to play the game,
or rather the cunning game, being played by the Mamas Mafia.
Apparently the treatment being dished out to Tom was nothing out
of the ordinary and it was something that all new traders had to
endure. Alonso explained that in order to supplement their meagre
state widows' pension, elderly female residents would loudly and
very publicly criticise a new trader's produce and then effectively
ostracise them until such time as that trader began to provide
them with free produce on an occasional basis.

'Over the years we have all had to take our turn,' Alonso had
told him, 'and as the new boy in town, it's currently yours.'

Tom was quick to heed the advice given to him by his fellow
trader. And from then on, whenever his produce was criticised by
a member of the Mamas Mafia, he did as all other market traders
had learned to do. He would offer an abject apology, beg for
forgiveness, swear by all that was Holy that he would never again
repeat this mortal sin and as a gesture of genuine contrition, offer
as much free produce as an elderly lady could carry in her wicker
basket.

Now playing the game, the demographic balance of his
customer base soon righted itself and a relieved Tom was able to
return home to Sarah with a pocketful of Euros, a bunch of flowers
- and very few lemons.

Although the unusually quiet streets of Funacaliente that
morning were puzzling Tom, on the plus side, they did enable
him to find a parking space right next to his destination of the
Town Hall with relative ease. As he parked his jeep at the foot of
the short flight of steps which led up to what was arguably the

most impressive and best maintained building in Funacaliente, Tom noticed a small knot of elderly and middle aged men deep in conversation at the top of the steps. One of the men was gesticulating wildly and was clearly annoyed about something. Tom turned the ignition key of his jeep to the off position and as the engine stumbled to a halt it gave its customary back fire which alerted the group of men to his arrival.

'Hola amigo,' said one of the younger members of the group to Tom as he climbed out of his vehicle.

'Hola Carlos,' replied Tom, looking up the steps and touching his temple with the forefinger of his right hand in a mock salute.

Carlos owned the farm on the other side of the ridge to Tom's finca and was perhaps his closest friend from the island's farming community. Being of a similar age to Tom and, like him, an escapee from a former life of stress and materialism, Carlos and Tom had grown to be firm friends over the last seven years. Carlos gestured with one of his muscular, chestnut brown arms for Tom to come and join them.

'Que passes?' said Tom, as he made his way up the flight of shining, black granite steps.

'Well, my friend, I'd like to say that all was well, but sadly I cannot.' Turning towards his companions, Carlos continued:

'You see, we didn't get our water this morning and as you might have gathered by now, none of us are particularly happy about it and some of us,' he said, looking in the direction of Pedro, 'are especially upset.'

Tom glanced at the man he had seen in a highly animated state when he had first arrived. Although Tom's Spanish was now almost perfect, he still found it difficult to understand the local dialect, especially when it was spoken rapidly. And as Pedro's words were coming incomprehensively thick and fast, Tom's quizzical look prompted Carlos to offer a quick translation.

'He's speculating about why his water didn't arrive this morning. He's convinced that this is just another attempt by the town's mayor to limit supplies and then force up the price and has nothing to do with last night's earthquake.'

Pedro, or El Toro, as he was called by his close friends owing to his large frame and ferocious temper, had fought for the Republican forces in the Civil War against Franco and, fifty years on, he still had a deep mistrust of any authority figure.

'Did you get your water?' enquired Carlos.

'No, not a drop,' said Tom. 'That's why I've come into town this morning.'

'Looks like last night's big earthquakes must have cracked the aqueduct on your side of the ridge as well then.'

'Earthquake, what's all this about an earthquake? ' said Tom, looking around him for signs of devastation and destruction; but the town's plaza looked much the same as ever, just quieter than normal.

'Amigo!' exclaimed Carlos, a slow grin beginning to form on his weather worn face, 'You must be either a really sound sleeper or perhaps had one bottle too many of vino last night. The first quake struck just after midnight and there were several, nearly as big, after- shocks for at least another hour after that.'

'Didn't hear or feel a thing,' said Tom, shaking his head in a slightly bemused manner.

'Holy Mary and Jesus, you must have heard it! That's why there's nobody around this morning. Everybody thinks the volcano, Teneguia, is waking up and there might be another eruption coming.'

Tom recalled his restless night's sleep and slowly it began to dawn on him that he might have been disturbed by an earthquake rather than by a thunderstorm or falling rocks.

'Just after midnight, you say. Actually, now you mention it, something did keep waking me up last night, but I thought it was just thunder or rock falls.'

'Si,' added Carlos. 'There's certainly been plenty of rock falls. Many of the local roads have been blocked, which is another reason why there are so few people in town today and I only just managed to get here myself.'

Tom remembered his own journey to town and an explanation for the unusually large number of rocks that he'd noticed on the "helter skelter" began to form in his mind. More worryingly, however, because of Carlos' comment about the volcano Teneguia, he also now had a possible explanation for the smell of sulphur that he had encountered that morning but he decided to keep that particular detail of his journey to himself - for a while at least, as the townsfolk were clearly already in a high state of anxiety and he didn't wish to be responsible for starting a widespread panic. *Besides*, he sought to convince himself, *a few brown trees and a whiff of sulphur doesn't spell an impending disaster, does it?*

As the sound of the town clock struck 8:00 a.m., the group of men all turned to face the imposing oak doors of the town hall and waited for them to be flung open. After five minutes and several sturdy thumps from Pedro's ham like fist on the door, it still hadn't opened, so Carlos reached for his mobile phone and called the number of the town hall. The phone rang and rang, but no one answered.

'There's nobody inside,' he reported back to the group of men.

'There must be,' said Pedro, his faced flushed with a mixture of effort from repeatedly banging on the door and frustration from getting no reply. 'I, for one,' he said, 'am not going anywhere until one of those corrupt money grabbing bastards comes out here and tells me where the hell my water is.'

The rest of the group nodded in agreement, apart from Carlos who announced that waiting on the steps was futile and that he was going to get some breakfast. He gestured for Tom to come and join him and, remembering that he had not eaten or drunk anything that morning, Tom decided to accompany Carlos to the small café located on the other side of the plaza.

The normally bustling café was, like the rest of the town that morning, almost empty when they walked in. Carlos winked at the attractive young waitress behind the counter and ordered two coffees.

'You're incorrigible,' said Tom to Carlos, who was still smiling and winking at the waitress.

Carlos raised his shoulders and, with the palms of his hands facing upward, adopted the posture that all Spaniards do when they are trying to act innocent and said,

'I know, but what else can a single man do to amuse himself in this town?'

Tom knew that Carlos' reference to his current marital status was actually him trying to make light of a personal tragedy that had actually brought him to La Palma, some ten years earlier. His wife had died from pancreatic cancer and for him La Palma was an escape, as it was for Tom, albeit for considerably less tragic reasons.

The waitress brought the two coffees over to their table and, predictably enough, Carlos seized the opportunity to give her another wink as he thanked her for their drinks. Tom couldn't be sure, but he got the distinct feeling that Carlos and the waitress knew each other and that this wasn't their first meeting because, as the waitress placed the two cups of coffee on their table, Carlos beckoned her to come closer so he could whisper something in her ear. And when she smiled coyly back at him before returning to her counter to serve another customer his suspicions were confirmed.

'See, I've still got it,' said Carlos.

'Amigo, like me the only thing you've got at the moment is a knackered back and an empty water tank,'

The smile on Carlos' face drained rapidly as he remembered the predicament they were both facing following the failure of their water allocation to arrive. Now alone with Carlos, Tom decided to broach the subject of last night's seismic activity and the possibility of another eruption.

'Tell me,' he said, 'what happened during the last eruption?'

A part smile, part smirk began to form on Carlos' face.

'Which one?' he replied, knowing that he had Tom at a distinct disadvantage regarding the island's volcanic history.

'There's been more than one?' said Tom, with a look of exaggerated horror on his face.

'Oh yes, my friend, Teneguia has been erupting throughout history,' and he began to reel off a long list of past eruptions.

'Phew!' said Tom, when Carlos eventually finished.'If I'd known I was coming to live on a time bomb I might have thought twice about settling here.'

'Don't worry, my friend, it only erupts every forty or so years and it's been quiet since it last woke up in 1971.'

Tom's mental arithmetic wasn't brilliant, but a quick calculation revealed that it had been over forty years since the last eruption.

'So, it's now a few years overdue!'

'Perhaps,' responded Carlos, 'But you know volcanoes don't erupt according to a strict timetable. It could be another hundred years before it decides to blow again.' Then, with the sly grin beginning to reform in the corners of his mouth, Carlos said, 'But then again, it could, of course, decide to blow tomorrow.'

Tom made a vain attempt to mask the anxiety that was clearly etched on his features.

'So tell me, what happened in the last eruption?'

Carlos' face darkened slightly.

'By Palmerian standards it was a big eruption and a bad time for local people, my friend, but nowhere near as bad as it could have been.'

Although he was tempted to have some fun at Tom's expense and greatly exaggerate the impact of the eruption, Carlos decided to spare his friend's feelings and to keep his account pretty much factual. 'Well,' he began, 'the first indication that something was happening came one Thursday in late October. At about midday, just as people were heading off for their afternoon siesta, a really big quake hit and it was felt all over the island. And, as it happens, the biggest tremor was felt right here, in this town and not surprisingly the locals were in a major state of panic.'

'Sounds vaguely familiar,' said Tom.

Carlos ignored Tom's interruption and continued, 'The tremors continued for much of that afternoon and on into the next day. At one point it was reported on the radio that four earthquakes a minute were happening and that night most of the population of the town and other nearby towns like Los Llanios spent the night in their cars or stayed out on the street.'

'Sounds terrible,' said Tom, who was secretly pleased that he had not been living on La Palma at that time.

'It was. Many of the town's older population remembered the last big eruption in 1949 and pretty soon the media started to speculate about the possibility of another eruption being imminent. Obviously, the locals were terrified and the whole town went into melt down.' Carlos paused for a moment and smiled briefly at his unintended witticism. 'Anyway, the minor quakes went on for about another twenty four hours without any let up and then, on the third night, there was one almighty quake, which according to locals, was so strong that it threw people from their beds and set all the bells in the town's churches ringing.'

Tom was momentarily reminded of his own disturbed sleep the night before.

'Then, almost as suddenly as they had started, the quakes stopped and for about a day or so all seemed to have returned to normal and the local people started to breathe a sigh of relief.'

'You say, *seemed* to have returned to normal,' said Tom. 'I take it then that there was still more to come.'

'Oh yes, amigo, the fireworks still hadn't started yet.' Carlos allowed himself a second small smile at another unintended witticism. 'You see we were now entering a period of what scientists called 'Harmonic Tremor.'

Tom had never heard of the term before and the bemused look on his face prompted Carlos to explain further. Carlos reached for a pencil in the top pocket of his shirt, and holding it horizontally between the thumb and forefinger of each hand, said 'Imagine that this pencil is the crust of the earth and my thumbs are molten rock rising up from below and exerting pressure on the crust.'

Tom nodded that he understood and gestured for Carlos to continue.

Carlos increased the pressure on the underside of the pencil and it began to bend ever so slightly.

'OK, now listen carefully,' instructed Carlos. 'Can you hear it?'

Tom listened as Carlos pushed his thumbs even harder against the pencil and the faint cracking and splintering of wood could now be heard.

'Hear that?'

Tom nodded again.

'There's your minor earthquakes, just like those that occurred in the days leading up to the eruption. Now keep watching and listening.'

The pencil was now discernibly bending as Carlos continued to exert pressure with his thumbs and the sound of cracking became even louder.

'Can you hear the bigger quakes?'

Tom nodded again, his eyes focused intently on the distorted pencil. Suddenly, and without any warning, there was a loud crack and the pencil broke into two.

'And there,' said Carlos triumphantly, waving both parts of the fractured pencil about in the air, 'is the really big quake just before the volcanic eruption.'

'And what about the harmonic tremor?'

'Ah, that's a bit trickier to explain,' said Carlos. 'All I know is that once the crust has cracked open the magma begins to rise and as it does it causes more quakes, but they tend to be smaller and less violent than the jerking and jolting ones which occurred before. It seems like everything is dying down, but that's far from what is really happening. It's a bit like the calm before a storm.'

Tom looked puzzled once again.

'Hey, give me a break will you. I'm only a burnt out sales executive not a geologist, you know. You really need to Google it for yourself if you want a more scientific explanation.'

Tom smiled and said 'I get the gist, but what happened once the eruption started?'

A sad look came over Carlos' face.

'Several weeks of hell, my friend, followed by months, maybe years, of fear and disruption. Red hot ash from the eruption covered the surrounding villages, burning everything it touched. Whole villages were evacuated. Some were destroyed. All the vineyards and banana plantations were ruined and many farmers went bust overnight and had to move away to Santa Cruz in order to find work. Local beaches turned black and lava flows spewed out from the crater into the sea, nearly destroying the local fishing fleet.'

'And the death toll?' asked Tom.

Carlos' face lightened slightly. 'Luckily, only two people died. But at one point it was feared that the mix of lava flows and sea water would cause a huge explosion so everyone in the area had to be evacuated.'

Carlos slumped back in his chair and Tom realised he had finished his account.

'You know something, my friend,' said Tom, in an attempt to lighten the sombre atmosphere. 'You would have made a bloody good teacher.'

Carlos laughed loudly and the handful of other customers in the café turned to look at him.

'And end up like you,' he said, laughing loudly again. 'Thanks, but no thanks, amigo.'

Suddenly, Carlos stopped laughing and a serious look came over his face again.

'What's the matter?' said Tom,

Reaching across the table, Carlos grasped Tom's arm, and said, 'I've just realised something.'

'Realised what?' asked Tom, still perplexed by his friend's rapid change in demeanour.

'Do you know what Funacaliente means in Spanish?'

Tom thought about the question for a few seconds before responding, 'Not really.'

'It means the place of the warm fountain.'

'And? ' said Tom, with a slight hint of exasperation in his voice.

'Where is the fountain in Funacaliente today?'

Tom looked out onto the plaza in front of the café where a large stone fountain was located.

'It's there,' he said pointing towards it.

'And have you ever seen water, let alone warm water, flowing from it?' asked Carlos.

'Now you mention it, no, never.'

'Precisely,' exclaimed Carlos, 'it stopped flowing just before the last eruption in 1971.

And do you know why it stopped flowing?'

Tom shrugged his shoulders.

'The spring which fed the fountain stopped flowing because the rising magma evaporated all the water in the underground aquifers and, once superheated, it turned the whole mountain into a pressure cooker which eventually blew its top.'

Tom was about to ask where Carlos was going with this point when he remembered the failure of his water allocation to arrive earlier that day and he, too, suddenly went very quiet.

Gradually, a possible explanation for their current water supply problems began to form simultaneously in the minds of both men. Perhaps, just perhaps, something far more dangerous than a localised earthquake or a corrupt local official was at the root of it all.

Chapter 12

United States Geological Survey, Virginia, USA

'Have you seen this print out?' Ross asked his colleague, Geoff Collins.

'Yes, I have, and it looks like we've had some overnight action under El Heirro. Could be that the magma chamber is stirring again.'

'Maybe,' said Ross, his attention still firmly focused on the mass of data which covered the computer print-out on the desk in front of him.'But let's hope not, because the last time that sucker stirred, I ended up on double shifts for a fortnight.'

'Yes, but just think about the overtime pay,' countered Geoff. 'And, if I remember correctly, that fortnight's overtime paid for your little jaunt over to Hawaii and we all know what happened there, don't we, Ross?'

Ross smiled as he remembered his chance meeting with a beautiful Spanish volcanologist who was in Hawaii on a two month secondment from the University of Madrid.

'Are you still in contact with her?' asked Geoff, more out of politeness than genuine interest.

'Nah, ships that pass in the night,' responded Ross, knowing full well that only last week he had emailed her. 'Holiday romance, that's all it was. Nothing more, nothing less,' he said, drawing the computer print-out closer to his face in an attempt to hide a sly smile.

'Shame,' said Geoff, who by now had detected Ross' fruitless attempt to hide his grin. 'Don't suppose you still have an email address for her as I wouldn't mind making her acquaintance, if, as you say, there's nothing happening between you and her these days?'

His question got the response it was designed to achieve, with Ross quickly raising his head from the print-out and flashing a look of annoyance at Geoff.

'Thought as much. Still got a 'hot spot' for her then, it would seem.'

'Do you think we could focus on the important stuff for a minute and not my sex life,' said Ross, his annoyance at Geoff's suggestion and enquiries into his personal life now quite visible.

'OK, OK,' said Geoff, realising that his probing and goading had gone a fraction too far. 'Let's get a visual image of the data and see what that tells us.'

For several minutes both volcanologists silently surveyed the series of images showing recent tremors within the Canary Islands before Ross broke the silence.

'Same old, same old if you ask me. Lots of small quakes with deep seated foci. Nothing out of the ordinary there and certainly nothing worthy of alarm.'

'What about that cluster of larger quakes in the centre of the El Heirro?' asked Geoff.

Ross zoomed in on the area of the island where three slightly larger red dots were located. He hovered the cursor over one of the red dots and an information tab suddenly appeared revealing the magnitude and depth of the quakes.

'5.1 on the Richter scale; that's a relatively large quake for the area,' remarked Ross.

'Sure is,' responded Geoff, ' but there no evidence of harmonic tremor, so it looks like the magma chamber is stable, plus the data from tilt meters stationed at Restinga are not indicating any swelling or deformation.'

Ross agreed that an eruption did not look imminent on El Heirro and both concluded that there was no need to issue any kind of alert. All was well at the moment on El Heirro and Ross was secretly pleased as that was where the Spanish volcanologist that he had met in Hawaii was currently based.

'What about the other islands?' asked Geoff.

After checking Gran Canaria and Lanzarote, Ross switched images on his computer screen and a map of La Palma flashed into view.

'Bit of small scale submarine activity to the south of the island and some…..'

Ross stopped talking momentarily and then continued, 'Now that's a bit more interesting.'

He pointed to the linear cluster of larger quakes along the Cumbre Vieja ridge.

'Pretty shallow too. I think we need to keep an eye on that little lot, don't you?'

'Most definitely,' said Geoff. 'What does the data from the tilt meters in that area indicate?'

Ross quickly surveyed the image showing localised crustal deformation.

'Nothing out of the ordinary, so it doesn't look like there's any upward movement in the magma chamber. But radon gas emissions are raised, although that's probably from the spate of recent seismic activity.'

'Could be,' said Geoff, with a note of uncertainty in his voice. 'But I think we should email Professor Stevens nevertheless and apprise him of the situation, don't you?'

'For sure', replied Ross. 'I don't want that sucker kickin' off on my watch without anyone else further up in the food chain knowing what we've seen. Leave it with me and I'll email him.'

As Geoff began walking away, Ross pressed the compose tab on his email account and began searching through his list of contacts. When he came to Professor Steven's email address he didn't pause, but continued scrolling down until he came to the contact name that he was really looking for. Then, when he was certain that his colleague was sufficiently far enough away, he began to write his message which began: Dear Maria,

Chapter 13

The Instituto Geografica Nacional, Frontera, El Heirro

Day 2

When Maria eventually arrived at work she was surprised to find the professor waiting in her office.

'You're late,' he said, in his characteristically brusque manner.

As she walked across the room towards where he was seated, the professor momentarily considered telling her how concerned he had been for her safety, but not wishing to sound like an over protective father, opted not to.

'I know, I am really late,' Maria began to say, but before she could offer him any further explanation, he interrupted her.

'Well, at least you're here now. So let's make a start on analysing last night's seismic activity.'

Three years ago, when Maria first arrived at the Institute, she had found the professor's abrupt manner quite upsetting, but nowadays she just accepted it as par for the course and tried to ignore it as much as she could.

'Of course,' she replied, reaching for the on button of her computer.

As she did so, the professor noticed the plasters on two fingers of her right hand. Once again, he was fleetingly tempted to enquire about her well-being, but chose to ignore the injury that she had presumably sustained during last night's quake, and focused instead on the image that sprung into view on her computer screen.

The professor pointed to the three red dots that he had noticed earlier. 'Two 5.1 and one 4.9 magnitude quakes.' he said. 'Quite close to your home, were they not?'

Maria's cursor hovered over the dots and confirmation of their magnitude and depth flashed into view.

'Yes, they woke me in the night,' and, sensing another opportunity to explain her late arrival, said, 'and they caused a major landslide on the road that I take to work each morning.' But the professor was not listening.

'Quite deep seated though, I see,' said the professor, referring to the depth of the quake's foci below the surface. 'Any shallower and I might have begun to fear for your safety, but at twelve kilometres deep I doubt there was any structural damage in your village or fatalities.'

'None that I'm aware of,' she said. 'Just a couple of cut fingers from picking up broken glass this morning before I left for work – that's all!'

Again he chose to ignore what was blatantly an attempt to explain her late arrival for work and, at the same time, a comment about his lack of concern for her safety.

'Is there any data available yet regarding crustal deformation in the area affected by the quakes?' asked Maria.

'I do believe there is,' he replied, with a hint of sarcasm in his voice. 'And I look forward to hearing all about it and your full report on every aspect of last night's quakes, in my office, at 2:00 p.m. today.' 'Oh, and by the way,' he added, 'try to be on time for once.'

As he turned to leave her office, the professor allowed himself a small smile and was still smiling when he returned to his own office, two minutes later.

As the sound of the professor's footsteps on the marble floor of the corridor became fainter and fainter, Maria felt sufficiently brave to quietly articulate her thoughts out loud.

'What's wrong with that man? I've worked with him for three years now and I don't even get a, 'Good morning, Maria', let alone a, 'thank God you're ok, Maria, I was really worried about you."

She knew the likelihood of the professor ever saying such things to her was an extremely remote one, but mocking him in this way made her feel a bit better nevertheless, especially as, in spite of his rude, arrogant and uncaring manner, she still found him irritatingly handsome and alluring.

Hastily suppressing such thoughts, Maria decided to quickly check the inbox of her email account before embarking on the task in hand. Her heart leapt slightly when she saw that she had a message from Ross who was the one man in her life who did appreciate her intellect, but her excitement quickly evaporated when she read its contents. It seemed clear that the professor had either forgotten to tell her, or perhaps had missed, God forbid, something about last night's activity, so she rapidly reloaded the page that she had been viewing with the professor. As she re-examined the pattern of coloured dots visible on the screen, her attention was drawn to an additional cluster of yellow and orange ones, on the sea bed, half way between El Heirro and La Palma, which Ross had mentioned in his email. The dots formed a line along a submarine fault running directly between the two islands. Closer to the coastline of La Palma the dots seemed to peter out and then, just north of the small town of Funacaliente, she saw something which made her heart race. All along the ridge known as Cumbre Vieja, which stretches from Funacaliente to the summit of the Caldera de Tabuiente, was a line of red dots and one purple one which Ross had suggested that she should keep under surveillance. As she moved her curser over each dot, the detail that was revealed about each one made her gasp out loud. 'My God,' she exclaimed. 'They're all 6.0 plus and all less than six kilometres deep!'

She switched to another website which gave data and digitalised images of ground deformation and radon gas emissions in that area. As it loaded, she silently prayed that the situation would be similar to that which Ross had described in his message and that there would be no evidence of the magma chamber under La Palma stirring. But her prayers went unanswered and the image that eventually emerged in front of her was now significantly more serious than Ross had said. She crossed herself, not once, but several times.

'Oh my God,' she murmured to herself. 'Holy Mother of Jesus, this looks bad.' Instantly, her thoughts switched to the safety of her parents.

A Palmerian by birth, Maria's parents had lived all their lives in the island's capital of Santa Cruz and potentially were now in grave danger. But as the enormity of what she was seeing on her computer screen began to sink in, she realised that so too was her sister who lived in Tenerife some miles to the south of La Palma. In fact, if what she was witnessing ran its possible nightmarish course, every inhabitant along the entire coastline of the Atlantic Ocean could be in great danger.

Maria did not wait for her 2:00 p.m. meeting with the professor. She ran, with tears in her eyes, as fast as the highly polished marble floors of the Institute's corridors would allow, straight to his office, and, without knocking, flung open the door. 'Professor!' she shouted, 'I think you shuold switch on your computer. There's something you need to see.'

But the professor was already looking at his computer screen and as he looked up and turned towards her she could see from the look on his face that he already knew what she had come to tell him. But she could also see from the glint in his eyes that rather than be worried by the potential danger that they were now all facing, the professor was actually excited by what was clearly developing.

'I know,' he said, 'but let's not jump to conclusions. This situation could play out in a hundred and one different ways, so let's not think too much about the worst case scenario – just yet, at least.'

In spite of his reassuring words, the professor could see the anxiety in Maria's eyes and, quite uncharacteristically, he rose from his desk and with outstretched arms beckoned her to come closer. She obediently complied and as his muscular arms enveloped her, she found the warmth of his body both comforting and at the same time rather exciting. And, although for a fleeting moment she felt safe in his arms, deep down she knew that they were far from safe and that their future, together with that of perhaps millions of people living along the entire length of the Atlantic Ocean, now hung in the balance.

Chapter 14

The US Geological Survey, Virginia, USA.

Professor Bill Stevens was a man of immense stature and even greater power. As Director General of the United States Geological Survey, he could, with just one phone call or an email, mobilise the country's National Guard or even order the evacuation of the entire population of the eastern seaboard of the USA. In fact, after the President, he was probably the second most powerful man in the entire nation. But the burden of such power and responsibility weighed heavily upon him and, as his predecessor had discovered, one wrong decision could spell the end of an otherwise unblemished career.

Consequently, Professor Stevens was not given to making rash or hasty decisions, but, when the need arose, he could act quickly and decisively, as he clearly demonstrated in the days leading up to the eruption of Mount St Helens some thirty years ago.

At that point in time, Professor Stevens had only just been appointed as Director General of the USGS and there were many who said that the thirty five year old, although a brilliant academic and highly respected volcanologist, was far too young to hold such a prestigious and important position. However, as a major eruption of Mount St Helens became increasing likely, he proved all his doubters wrong in one fell swoop by ordering the evacuation of over thirty-five thousand local residents and tourists - a move which unquestionably saved all of their lives because, when the volcano did eventually blow a few days later, it was a truly cataclysmic event.

The eruption of Mount St. Helens began with 5.1 magnitude quake. While there had been literally hundreds of earthquakes in the lead up to the eventual eruption, the unstable north face of the volcano could not sustain another, and within moments the largest landslide in recorded history removed more than thirteen hundred feet from the summit and swept away almost the entire north side of the mountain and what was once the ninth highest peak in Washington State was suddenly reduced to the thirtieth.

As the north face slid away, it let loose the trapped gases, just like a cork being removed from a well shaken bottle of champagne, and travelling at speeds nearing six hundred miles per hour and at a temperature of three hundred degrees centigrade, the blast of gas and pulverised rock flattened everything in its path for two hundred and thirty square miles to the north of the mountain.

Although Professor Stevens could do nothing to save the lives of the fifty nine people who, for one reason or another, refused to leave the danger area, or indeed anything about the ash cloud which the eruption created and its subsequent spread over much of North America, as a result of his quick and decisive actions he was hailed as a hero by all sections of the US media and, as such, his tenure as Director General of the USGS was secured – until now at least.

Of course, there were those in volcanology circles who argued that Professor Stevens had simply got lucky, and the professor would have been the first to admit, albeit privately, that the decision to evacuate the Mount St Helens area had not been a difficult one to make. In the months and weeks leading up to the eruption, the volcano had given plenty of precursors of what was going to happen. The biggest of these being the two hundred and

fifty metre high cryptodome or bulge which had grown on the
northern side of the volcano. For the informed this was more than
enough of a clue that the vent had become plugged with magma
and for these few the cataclysm which ensued was no more than
they expected.

Fortunately for Professor Stevens such major tectonic events
are a rare occurrence in the US and since the eruption of Mount
St Helens his judgement and decision making skills had not been
tested to the same degree. That was, of course, until he opened
the email from Ross. From its content about recent seismic
activity on La Palma, it was clear that the time for him to step up
to the plate was again upon him and the decision that he had long
dreaded having to make had just moved one step closer and, for
the first time in his career, he prevaricated.

Professor Steven's reluctance to act resulted from the
publication of research by British Geologists from the University
College London and because of this, the USGS had kept a watchful
eye on all seismic and volcanic activity on the island of La Palma
in the Canary Islands. The geologist's research indicated that a
huge lump of rock, the size of the Isle of Man, could fall off La
Palma if its volcano, Cumbre Vieja, erupted and this could have
potentially devastating consequences for the east coast cities
of the USA. Although scientific opinion was divided as to the
likelihood of this ever happening, given the impact that this mega-
slide could potentially have on the USA, the USGS had secretly
formulated a contingency plan which essentially entailed the
complete evacuation of the population of the eastern seaboard of
the USA. This dramatic course of action was deemed necessary
because the British Geologists postulated that a mega-slide would
trigger giant waves called mega-tsunamis. Travelling at speeds
of up to six hundred miles per hour, these huge walls of water
would tear across the Atlantic Ocean smashing into islands and

continents and leaving a trail of death and destruction in their wake.

The geologist's computer models of the island's collapse showed that the first regions to be hit, with waves topping one hundred metres, would be the neighbouring Canary Islands and, within a few hours, the west coast of Africa would be battered with similar-sized waves. Between nine and twelve hours after the island collapsed, waves between twenty and fifty metres high would have raced across four thousand miles of the Atlantic Ocean to crash into the Caribbean islands and then the eastern seaboard of the US and Canada. The worst-hit areas would be harbours and estuaries, which would channel the waves inland and the loss of life and destruction to property would probably be immense with at least one hundred million people at risk.

The evacuation plan that the USGS had formulated listed those areas and cities along the eastern seaboard which would be hit first and estimated the likely death toll in each one.

Florida would probably be the first to succumb to the mega-tsunami. The cities of Miami and Jacksonville, given their location at sea level, would be completely inundated and a death toll of about one million would be highly likely. Opinion about what would happen to those cities surrounding the Gulf of Mexico was, however, divided. Some argued that the Floridian peninsular would act as a buffer to the tsunami and it would be deflected northwards, along the eastern seaboard of the US. Others maintained that the huge volume of water entering the Gulf would become trapped within it, and the tsunami would regrow in height to approximately one hundred and fifty metres. The low lying Mississippi delta region would be completely swamped and the cities of Baton Rouge and New Orleans virtually wiped from the map. Houston, at the far end of the Gulf, would also be badly hit and it was predicted that the likely death toll in the Gulf States alone would be in the region of ten million.

The mega-tsunami would then work its way inexorably northwards, inundating and completely devastating the coastal plains of every state from Georgia in the south to Maine in the north. The cities of Savannah and then Charleston would be hit next with an expected loss of life of three million. Wilmington, Greenville and Norfolk, with a combined population of 1 million, would be next in line for inundation, but the death toll would rocket to the tens of millions when the tsunami reached the densely populated coastal fringes of Delaware, Maryland and New Jersey.

Funnelled and constricted by the geography of the area into the estuaries of the Potomac and Delaware rivers, the tsunami would once again grow in height to one hundred metres and would devastate the cities of Baltimore and Philadelphia and then move on to New York, where, just in this one city, somewhere in the region of eight million people would be at risk.

The geologist's prediction was not without precedent as, throughout geological history, mega-slides such as the one they were predicting had occurred on neighbouring islands and, as recently as 1949, when La Palma's volcano Cumbre Vieja last erupted, a huge section of its western flank dropped four metres into the ocean. Most worryingly of all, according to the geologists, this chunk of land was still slipping slowly into the Atlantic Ocean, but if there was another eruption, the entire western flank could collapse in less than ninety minutes.

As nothing could be done to prevent the passage of these mega-waves, the only course of action open to USGS would be the evacuation of all settlements which lay in their path. But here was the dilemma that Professor Stevens faced. An evacuation on this scale would have major economic and social implications in both the short and long term and if it turned out to be a false alarm –

well, that would have spelt the end of his career, as it had done for his predecessor who had issued a yellow alert and put the entire east coast on standby when La Palma's Teneguia volcano had erupted in 1971.

When the professor read the content of Ross' email, his mind filled with images of the chaos that would ensue if he decided to issue an alert, and the complete pandemonium that there would be if he went to the next level and ordered a full scale evacuation. Every Interstate along the entire eastern coast would be log jammed with people trying desperately to get to higher ground inland. Hospital staff would be desperately trying to get the sick and the elderly to safety, schools would be shut and residential areas would be deserted. Factories, ports and city centres would grind to a halt and then, of course, would come the looters, eager to take advantage of the situation. Images of shops burning, the air thick with tear gas and the flashing blue lights of police cars began to fill his thoughts. And then, amongst the wailing of police sirens, there would be the inevitable sound of rifle shots as police marksmen sought to stem the rising tide of public disorder. God forbid if, after all the disruption and mayhem that his order would undoubtedly precipitate, it turned out to be a false alarm. His reputation would be in tatters and his otherwise unblemished career would be over in the blink of an eye.

No, he ultimately concluded, at this point in time he would not risk his career by issuing a yellow alert and would delay any evacuation order until he was certain that Cumbre Vieja was about to collapse and a mega-tsunami inevitable. It was a gamble, but if all hell did break loose on La Palma, he would still have an eight hour window to issue an evacuation order and save the population of the east coast and, of course, his career.

But there was one thing he was certain of. He desperately needed more intelligence on what was happening on La Palma and the best person to gather that information was the man whose email he had just opened and read - Ross Macintyre. Professor Stevens reached for his phone and began to dial Ross' number and as he did so a feeling of déjà vu suddenly swept over him, because this was not the first time that he had called upon a member of his staff to report on a developing crisis. This time, however, he hoped that the outcome would be better than before as he didn't wish to be responsible for yet another young geologist's death.

Chapter 15

London, England

'Hey mum!' shouted Charlotte from the lounge, where she was watching the six o'clock news. 'You need to come and look at this - now!'

'I can't,' said Sarah, who was in the kitchen preparing the evening meal. 'What is it anyway?'

'It's La Palma, it's on the news.'

At the mention of the island's name, Sarah stopped what she was doing and, with her hands still covered in pizza dough, joined her daughter on the sofa, but the news item was just coming to an end.

'So what's happening there?'

Charlotte, who was Sarah's daughter by her first marriage, replied,

'All the tour companies are pulling people out of hotels in the south of the island and flying them back to England.'

'Whatever would they want to do that for?'

'Because,' continued Charlotte, 'of all the recent earthquakes there, that's why. Apparently, Los Llanios and Funacaliente have been quite badly shaken and scientists are worried that there could be worse to come.'

Sarah's thoughts drifted momentarily back to the times when, whilst living at the finca, she and Tom had experienced relatively small quakes and began to smile slightly when she recalled how

Tom would often ask her 'If the earth had moved for her last night in bed or was it just another quake on the ridge.'

'Why are you smiling, mum?' asked Charlotte. 'This is serious stuff.'

Sarah refocused her thoughts.

'They must have been pretty large if they're evacuating people.'

'I'm not sure of precisely how big they were, but I suspect it's probably just the tour companies over-reacting or trying to cover their arses.'

'Even so, it's fairly unusual to get big quakes in the Canaries. Have there been any casualties?'

'Information about that is still a bit sketchy,' replied Charlotte, 'but they interviewed some director or other from this organisation that monitors quakes and volcanic activity on the island and he said that they were dispatching a team of scientists to the area and they'd know more once they'd completed their assessment of the situation.'

Sarah's brow furrowed slightly.

'I think I'd best give Tom a ring and check that he's ok. That is, of course, if I can manage to get through to him.'

'You'd be best off texting him, mum, as you'll never get a connection if you ring.'

Even though she was estranged from Tom, she still thought about him often, cared for him and even missed him. And, just recently, had begun to have second thoughts about her decision to return to England, although her separation from Tom had little to do with her feelings in this respect. Finding work in the financial sector, post Leman and during a global recession, was proving to be more difficult than she had expected. Plus, there were some aspects of life on the farm that she was actually beginning to miss. Easier though it was, reaching into the fridge to get an egg for breakfast, it was nowhere near as satisfying as her daily battle to find and collect eggs on the farm had been. And, although she never, ever, thought she would think this way, she was actually missing that feeling of exhaustion that you can only get from having done a hard day's manual labour. In fact, since returning to England she had never once slept the night through, like she always did in Spain, and frequently found herself wandering around her daughter's flat in the early hours of the morning, too awake to sleep.

And then there was the view from her daughter's flat. A luxury apartment in a refurbished warehouse, overlooking a former dock-cum-marina, may well have been what today's young and upwardly mobile sections of the population aspire to, but, as far as she was concerned, it in no way matched the view from the ridge on which their farm was located.

But there was one further reason why she found herself considering a return to the island. It was a reason that only she knew, and Sarah often chastised herself for even thinking about it. After discovering what had brought him to the island, Sarah had become very close to Carlos and what had begun as a simple friendship with a neighbour had gradually developed into something more significant. Carlos had, in fact, come to La Palma from mainland Spain after his wife had died in 2001. He, too, had bought a run-down finca, but on the opposite side of the ridge to Tom and Sarah, and had lived there alone for three years prior to their arrival. Unlike Tom and Sarah's finca, Carlos' farm was close enough to the nearby town to be connected to the mains electricity supply and, in consequence, he had such luxuries as an electric shower and an automatic washing machine. These were two items from her former life that Sarah missed perhaps the most, and, when living in their finca got too much for her, she would often end up over at Carlos' house, using his facilities and, as he was always glad of the company, it was a perfect arrangement. But over time Sarah found herself becoming increasingly fond of Carlos, especially when he confided in her about his wife's suffering and his subsequent depression after her passing. Nothing had ever happened between them, but, if Tom had not been around, she knew, as did Carlos, that something probably would have and she sometimes found herself fantasising about what could have been if she had stayed on the island. And even now she still wasn't one hundred percent certain if it was her dislike of living without modern conveniences or fear about her developing feelings for Carlos that had made her leave the island. Consequently she often found herself considering returning to the island but, so far at least, the home comforts afforded by her daughter's duplex apartment in which she was now living had proved sufficiently seductive to push such thoughts quickly, although not entirely, from her mind.

Sensing her mother's concern about Tom's safety and completely unaware of any other possible motive that she might have for returning to La Palma, Charlotte suggested that Sarah should fly back out there.

'I'll even google British and Iberian Airways if you like and find out when the next flight is,' said Charlotte.

'Oh, that's charming, that is,' replied Sarah. 'Whilst every other Brit is being flown *off* the island, you're after sending me *into* the disaster zone.' And then added, 'But then again, it would get me out of your hair, wouldn't it?'

Charlotte raised her hands in a show of mock horror. 'Mother, that's the furthest thing from my mind,' she said, trying hard to disguise a small tell-tale grin. 'I just don't want you worrying, that's all.'

But secretly Charlotte would have been delighted to get her mother on the next plane to La Palma. Since leaving university deep in debt six years ago, Charlotte had worked like a Trojan trying to set up an online clothing business and, after struggling initially, her business had gone from strength to strength. In fact, things were now going so well that she had recently been able to afford to buy her own flat outright and was over the moon when she was able to put the days of house sharing behind her until, of course, her mother reappeared on the scene.

Now aged twenty seven, independent and successful, Charlotte didn't want a parent waiting up for her after she'd had a night out with friends. Or asking her what time she would be home for dinner, or, indeed, what she wanted for dinner. That had been fine when she was a teenager, living at home and dependent on her parents, but that was then, and this was her time now and, what's more, this was her house and she didn't need or want to be answerable to anyone, however well - meaning they were.

Sarah pondered her daughter's suggestion for a few moments longer and then announced,

'Alright, I'll do it, but God knows what sort of reception I'll get from Tom when I arrive.'

How Charlotte managed to supress a cheer when Sarah announced her decision she would never know, but within thirty minutes she had booked and paid for her mother's flight to La Palma and, if she could have done, would have helped her to pack her bags as well.

'I think it might be a good idea if you actually texted him, rather than just turning up unannounced,' said Charlotte.

Sarah agreed that a warning text would be a good idea and went to get her phone from her hand bag. But it wasn't just Tom that she sent a text to; she also sent one to Carlos, informing him of her plans to come back and, unlike her message to Tom, she ended his with a kiss.

Chapter 16

The Instituto Geografica Nacional, Frontera, El Heirro

Day 2

The helicopter that the professor had requested to take him and Maria to La Palma arrived precisely on time and landed in the rear car park of the institute. Usually it would have taken him several days of beaurocratic wrangling to get approval for the deployment of the Institute's only helicopter and its use was generally limited to those occasions when the team needed to access a remote site which was inaccessible by road. On this occasion, however, although Cumbre Vieja could be reached via a dirt track, the information that he had emailed to the Institute's Director General just three hours ago about the current seismic activity on La Palma was sufficiently serious to warrant him cutting through the red tape and instantly approving the despatch of the helicopter.

Although the placement of several seismic monitoring stations, tilt meters and radon gas monitors on La Palma following the eruption of Teneguia some years earlier yielded highly valuable real time data about the developing situation on the island, the helicopter had been requested by the professor because there was no substitute for, as he liked to put it, 'Feeling the eruption through the soles of your feet,' and he often said to Maria, 'You have to get up close and personal to the volcano if you want to really understand it. You have to listen to its heartbeat and smell its breath if you are going to have any idea what it's planning to do.'

The professor's preferred methods of studying volcanoes was not without its dangers and this daredevil attitude was one that he had nurtured whilst working with the husband and wife team of Maurice and Katia Krafft some years earlier. The Kraffts were world famous volcanologists and as a young undergraduate, some thirty years ago, the professor had been seconded to work with them at the University of Paris. The professor had accompanied the Kraffts to some of the most violent and dangerous eruptions on the planet and the asbestos suit and steel helmet that he wore to protect himself from the red hot gases and falling lava bombs which ordinarily hung proudly in his office, were now swaying gently in the rear of the helicopter as he and Maria took off and headed for La Palma. But this was not the only memento that he still had from his days working with the Kraffts. The slight limp that the professor had was actually the result of a severely broken leg he had sustained during an expedition with the Kraffts to the eruption of the Redoubt Volcano in Alaska, in 1989. Ironically, this injury had prevented him from accompanying Maurice and Katia on their next expedition to Mount Unzen, Japan, and, as it transpired, was instrumental in saving the professor's life.

On the day before the eruption of Mount Unzen, Maurice was reported to have said to the press, 'If I die tomorrow, then I will die a happy man because I have spent my life studying what I love most.'

These proved to be prophetic words as he, his wife Katia, and thirty nine other volcanologists and journalists were all killed the next day by an avalanche of red hot rock and gas travelling at two hundred miles per hour, known as a pyroclastic flow. This avalanche of death had swept down the flanks of Mount Unzen in the direction that the Kraffts had predicted until, at the last second, it had switched course and headed for the area where the

Krafft's expedition was located. Katia's body was never recovered, but Maurice's body was found not long after the tragedy and identification was made simple by the fact that the heat of the pyroclastic flow had instantaneously evaporated every drop of water in his body and had effectively turned him into a piece of charcoal, with all his features perfectly intact.

Since the Kraffts' demise, the professor had become considerably more cautious when visiting an eruption, but nothing would ever completely quash his desire to get as close as possible to an eruption and now his assistant, Maria, was about to experience, for the first time in her short career, the adrenalin filled type of volcanology that the professor was completely and utterly addicted to.

Chapter 17

Granja en los Pinos, La Palma

Day 2

Tom's mind was full of troubled thoughts as he drove back to the finca. No water was one thing, but a possible volcanic eruption was another, much more worrying, problem. On the drive he had tried to console himself with the fact that Carlos was not a scientist and that his prediction was probably just pure speculation. Granted, he clearly knew more about the island's troubled volcanic past than he did, and he certainly seemed well informed about the whole business of volcanic eruptions, but, at the end of the day, he was still just a burned out insurance executive, with, it must be said, an inherent fascination for risks and disasters. After all, that had been his business for most of his working life – spreading doom and gloom and frightening people into buying his company's over- priced insurance policies.

Nonetheless, the picture that Carlos had painted, exaggerated or not, was a pretty worrying one and it played heavily on his mind for the entire journey. And it became even more so when, for the second time that day, he had smelt sulphur as he drove along the ridge to his farm. If anything, he thought, *the smell was considerably stronger now and not just the occasional whiff, but pretty much continuous.*

His concerns deepened still further when he drove through

the rustic gate of his farm. Ordinarily he would have been greeted by Daisy, barking wildly in celebration at his return home, but she was still nowhere to be seen.

Tom parked his jeep and called her name, but she still failed to appear. Perplexed, Tom walked across to the barn where she slept at night. The inside of the barn was dark and, having just come in from the blinding sunlight, it took his eyes a few minutes to adjust to the gloomy interior. He directed his gaze to where Daisy normally slept, but there was no sign of her there.

'Daisy, Daisy, where the hell are you, dog?' he called.

Then, from the deepest recesses of the barn, he heard a simpering sound and low whine and then saw, cowering behind a pile of old sacks, his missing companion.

'Ah, there you are!' he exclaimed, jubilantly. 'What's wrong with you, old girl?'

Half crawling, half squirming, but thankfully with her tail wagging furiously, Daisy made her away across the floor of the barn. Although still whining slightly, she was clearly pleased to see him and, in true Collie fashion, momentarily lost control of her bladder and a small pool of urine began to form on the floor of the barn.

'Whatever is the matter with you?' he said, as he rubbed her ruff with both hands. 'Come on, let's get you some food'

As Tom stood up and turned to leave the barn, he half expected to see Daisy excitedly dash past him in the direction of the finca's kitchen. Food, chasing rabbits and travelling in his jeep were the things that excited Daisy more than anything else on Earth, but on this occasion she stayed by his side, crouching and clearly terrified by something or other. Tom couldn't work out what was wrong with her, but for the rest of that day she stayed glued to him and, most strangely of all, didn't touch one morsel of her breakfast.

But Daisy was not the only animal behaving out of character that morning. Sarah's chickens were also conspicuous by their absence. By this time of the day they normally would have been busily scratching the ground of the finca's courtyard or wandering in and out of the kitchen looking for Sarah with the bag of seed that she invariably had secreted about her person. But the chickens were still in the henhouse and seemed unwilling to leave, even when he tried to shoo them outside.

Taking a seat on the bench that he had also made from wood found scattered around the farm, Tom's thoughts turned to his wife again and, as he imagined her wandering around the courtyard, scattering seed and calling her chickens, a feeling of sadness began to wash over him and memories of the happier times that they had enjoyed together when they first arrived at Granja en los Pinos began to fill his thoughts.

Their new home had been a long neglected farm house known locally as a finca. Located high up on the southern side of Cumbre Vieja, lacking electricity, running water and several kilometres from the nearest village, Granja en los Pinos was precisely what Tom had been looking for. In his opinion it was a rural paradise, but for Sarah their new home eventually came to represent a rural hell. Granted there were lemon trees in abundance and even an olive grove, but a fridge to chill her tonic water and a shady patio upon which she could read her book and take her afternoon siesta, were all sadly lacking and were never, in spite of Tom's best efforts, ever to materialise.

Sensing her bitter disappointment when they first set eyes on Granja en los Pinos, Tom did what he always did on such occasions. He quickly and excitedly described all the changes that he would soon be making in order to make their new home more comfortable and, for a while at least, Sarah was appeased and agreed to give their new life a go.

Despite their differing expectations of living life away from the 'rat race', one thing which they both did agree on was the spectacular view from their new home. Situated some six hundred metres above sea level, the deep blue Atlantic Ocean was clearly visible above the tops of the pine trees which cloaked the steep slopes of the ridge. Way below them was the Los Llanios valley where the Taburiente River could be just seen snaking its way to the Atlantic Ocean through villages of white washed houses, deep green banana plantations and groves of lemon and olive trees. On the far side of the valley, vineyard after vineyard were stacked, seemingly on top of one another, on the terraced slopes that formed the lower part of the ridge.

And then there were the aromas of the Palmarian Mountains. Each day, just before noon, when the heat of the sun had sufficiently warmed the tree clad flanks of the ridge, the intoxicating smell of pine resin and juniper berries, borne on zephyrs rising from the valley floor, would waft up to meet them, infusing the air around the finca and their senses with a heady concoction. At night, especially moonlit ones, the view took on a magical quality and the scents of summer were even more powerful and pungent. The distant river appeared now like a thread of silver silk which had been casually cast onto the deep purple, velvet floor of the valley and, when lit by moonlight, the tops of the pine trees resembled a dark green army, with thousands upon thousands of shining, silver spear heads, all pointing skywards. Whatever their new home lacked in modern conveniences, it certainly made up for it with its location – in Tom's opinion at least.

True to his word, during their first year in residence, life at Granja en los Pinos did become marginally more comfortable. The purchase of a petrol driven generator from a neighbouring farmer gave them light at night, and a wood burning oven, bought at a local market, plus the installation of some rudimentary plumbing, made daily ablutions and other domestic tasks considerably easier.

However, Sarah soon discovered that washing her clothes in an old galvanised bath tub filled with lukewarm water took much longer and required considerably more effort than flicking a switch and turning a dial on her Hotpoint washing machine. Similarly, and much to her dismay, Sarah also soon discovered that chickens do not always provide eggs at the precise time that they are needed. Nor, for that matter, do they always lay them where you'd expect them to and her arms invariably bore the scratches and cuts of abortive attempts to recover an egg which had been carefully, but most inconveniently, laid under a thorn bush or on the uppermost beam in the roof of an old lean-to which doubled as a henhouse.

But above all, and from the point of view of her happiness and continued residence in their new home, Sarah soon came to realise that laying on a sun lounger, with a book in one hand and a gin and tonic in the other, was something that people on holiday did; and life at their new home was far from a holiday. In fact, the only time that she got to lay down and read was at night, providing, of course, that the generator hadn't run out of petrol. Even then, she was usually so exhausted from chopping wood for the stove or hauling buckets of water across the courtyard, that she had no energy to read and usually fell asleep as soon as her head hit the pillow.

And wonderful though it was, eventually the view from their finca no longer compensated for the lack of creature comforts, and Sarah began to feel that living in their rural backwater was totally intolerable. And so it came as no surprise to Tom when Sarah suddenly announced, one morning some six months ago, that, 'enough was enough' and that she was leaving him and returning to England and "civilisation".

The sound of a helicopter chattering overhead suddenly dragged Tom from his daydream. Shielding his eyes from the blinding sun, Tom struggled to see the markings on the craft's fuselage and he couldn't make out if it was the Air Sea Rescue helicopter, which occasionally flew over, or one from the nearby military base. As the helicopter drew closer it became apparent that it was neither, and Tom was unsure what the initials GIS, which were emblazoned on its side, stood for.

The helicopter carrying the professor and Maria swooped low over Granja en los Pinos, circled twice, and then landed in a maelstrom of dust and leaves some three hundred metres along the ridge from Tom's farm. The noise of its arrival caused the chaffinches - which had been unusually quiet earlier that morning - to suddenly begin chattering noisily and then take off from their roosting place in a nearby juniper tree, in a highly agitated dark brown cloud of feathers, disturbed insects and dust. Daisy was also highly excited by the helicopter's arrival and, momentarily forgetting what had frightened her during the night, abandoned Tom's side and began running wildly around the finca's courtyard, barking loudly at the noisy intruder and nipping at the chickens who had now also ventured from their hen house.

As the rhythmically swishing rotor blades slowed, and the noise of the helicopter's engine began to fade, Tom rose from the bench and, perplexed by the helicopter's arrival, began making his way towards it. As he drew closer, Tom was quick to notice the female passenger who was first to emerge from the rear of the craft. Dressed in a figure hugging bright orange flight suit, Maria was a welcome, but nonetheless unusual sight for Tom, whose farm was rarely visited by anyone, let alone an attractive young woman. Tom was intrigued and his initial feelings of annoyance at having had the peace and tranquillity of his remote home disturbed by these uninvited visitors quickly began to ebb away.

Spotting Tom's approach, Maria smiled broadly, raised one arm and shouted the customary greeting,

'Hola'

By now Tom was close enough to see just how stunningly attractive Maria actually was. Her shoulder length, wavy, black hair, deep brown eyes and tanned complexion immediately identified her as probably Spanish; a fact that was confirmed when she began to introduce herself and the professor, who was now standing beside her.

'Bueno día, señor . Yo soy María Gonzales y este es mi colega , professer Felipe de Costa'

Although perfectly capable of continuing the conversation in Spanish, Tom decided to reply in English.

'What can I do for you?' he said, with a slight hint of distrust in his voice.

With his dark hair and deeply tanned face and arms, Tom looked like a typical Palmarian farmer and Maria and the professor were slightly taken aback to learn that he was not Spanish. But as they both spoke fluent English and sensing the less than cordial tone in Tom's voice, Maria decided to try and placate him by continuing the conversation in English.

'We are sorry to disturb you, señor,' Maria began apologetically. 'But we are here on a matter of great national, perhaps international, importance.'

'International importance?' said Tom, who was now more confused than annoyed.

'How the hell can my small farm be of international importance? Who precisely are you?' asked Tom.

Maria continued, 'We are Earth scientists from the Instituto Geografico Nacional which is based on El Heirro and we are here to conduct some routine investigations into......'

'Routine investigations into what exactly?' interrupted Tom.

Maria turned towards the professor as she was unsure as to whether or not she should divulge the exact nature of their visit to La Palma.

The professor nodded for Maria to continue.

'We are here to investigate some recent seismic activity in this area and, with your permission, we would like establish a base camp on your farm and survey the terrain from here up to the summit of Cumbre Vieja.'

'And what, precisely, do you expect to find?' asked Tom.

'Well, señor, perhaps some small changes in the shape of the land or any evidence that would suggest that a ....', Maria's voice trailed away and, once again, she looked to the professor for a sign that she should say more.

Sensing her uncertainty, the professor joined the conversation.

'Señor, what my colleague is basically trying to say is that you are possibly in great danger and we would advise you to consider leaving the area as quickly as possible.'

'Leave my home! Danger? What danger? I can't see any danger!' said Tom, turning his body through three hundred and sixty degrees and looking all around. 'Unless, of course, you consider the odd rock fall to be sufficiently dangerous to warrant abandoning my home,' he continued, making no attempt to hide the sarcasm in his voice.

'Señor, you are looking in the wrong place,' said the professor. 'The danger you are in is not visible at present, because it lies out of sight, beneath your feet.'

Tom was slightly taken aback by the professor's reply. Moreover, from the look on his visitors' faces, it was obvious that they were genuinely concerned about his safety and it was at that point that he remembered the strange sights and smells that he had encountered en route to Funacaliente and the conversation that he had had with Carlos earlier in the day. Suddenly, the pieces of the jigsaw began to fall somewhat worryingly into place.

'Are you trying to tell me that there might be some kind of volcanic eruption about to happen?' asked Tom impatiently.

Both scientists nodded simultaneously.

'Well in that case, I think.' said Tom gravely, 'you'd best join me back at the farm because I have some information that may be of some use to you.'

Once seated around Tom's kitchen table, he began to relate some of the strange sights and odours that he had noticed whilst driving into town earlier that day. He started by describing the unusually large number of rocks on the track and the lack of bird song, but none of this seemed to particularly interest either of the two scientists. But mention of the smell of sulphur and misaligned trees instantly grabbed their attention.

'You say the trees seemed to be pointing at an angle, downslope?' said the professor, his body now leaning towards Tom's.

'And the tree's foliage was more brown than green?' asked Maria.

Tom nodded again and added that the trees appeared to be more dead than alive.

Maria and the professor momentarily shared a knowing look which went unnoticed by Tom who had been distracted by the sound of Daisy, whining somewhere outside in the courtyard.

'And', asked Maria, 'did you notice any unusual bulges or raised areas on the hillside?'

Still partially distracted by Daisy's continued whining, Tom shook his head, and asked,

'Why? Is that significant then?'

'Crustal deformation is always significant,' said the professor, 'especially when combined with increased gas emissions as it indicates that magma is possibly rising within the crust.'

The image of Carlos bending the pencil in the café earlier that day instantly flashed into Tom's mind.

'And that means an eruption is imminent, I suppose,' said Tom.

'Quite possibly,' said the professor. 'But equally, it could simply mean that the magma chamber is just restless and, after some initial upward movement, it could settle again and the chance of an eruption may well diminish.' 'But,' he continued, 'before we can say with any degree of certainty what is likely to happen, we need to make some first - hand observations, which is why we are here and, I repeat, that it would be safer if you evacuated your home.'

'I appreciate your concern,' said Tom, and then, with his eyes fixed firmly on Maria's face, added, 'But you said earlier that this matter may well be an issue of international concern and I get the distinct feeling that you are not telling me the whole story.'

Maria and the professor exchanged a glance that instantly confirmed to Tom that his suspicions were well founded.

The professor was first to reply.

'You are right, señor, this could well become a much bigger matter than I have outlined, but the chances of that happening are extremely slim.'

'Precisely how big a matter?' asked Tom.

'I really would prefer not to say at this point,' replied the professor, 'because it is only a remote possibility and it may well never happen again on this island.'

'What may never happen again?' said Tom, with a rising note of exasperation in his voice.

Uncharacteristically, the professor's voice faltered slightly, as he too was now unsure as to whether or not he should divulge the exact enormity of what might be happening on La Palma, but a nod from Maria signalled that he should continue.

'How well do you know La Palma's sister island of El Heirro?' asked the professor.

'Not that well,' replied Tom.

At this point, the professor took a pen and scrap of paper from his pocket and drew a rough outline of the island of El Heirro. Pointing to each of the three huge bays which characterise the island's coastline, he asked Tom if he had any idea how these features may have been formed.

Memories of his O level Geography teacher's explanation of coastal bay formation filtered into his mind and Tom replied, 'Coastal erosion, perhaps.'

The professor smiled and somewhat patronisingly told Tom that coastal erosion was a good guess, but not correct, and then continued, 'Let me tell you, señor, what has happened on El Heirro during the last five hundred thousand or so years. Following major volcanic eruptions, there is evidence of at least three major landslides on El Heirro, and by major landslides I do not mean a few tonnes of rocks and mud sliding into the sea. I am talking about whole sections of the island slipping into the sea; landslides which were large enough to create tsunamis which must have devastated coastlines perhaps hundreds or maybe even thousands of miles away. The most recent of these was the 'El Golfo' landslide that occurred about fifteen thousand years ago and involved the collapse of the northern flank of the island. The landslide formed the El Golfo Bay and created a debris avalanche with a volume of one hundred and eighty km^3. Big enough to create waves at least one hundred feet high and travelling at speeds in the region of six hundred miles per hour.'

'And you say that these landslides were triggered by a volcanic eruption?' said Tom.

'Well yes,' said the professor, 'but it was a probably a single vent eruption on El Heirro. And that's a different situation to what might happen here, on La Palma. If anything, an eruption on this island will probably cause a much bigger landslide – a mega-slide, in fact, to use a geomorphological term.'

'Why is that then?' said Tom, clearly not understanding why it should be so much worse on La Palma.

'The type of eruption on La Palma,' said Maria, taking up the explanation, 'could possibly be an interlocking vent eruption. This could result in a fissure several miles long opening up along the ridge and the simultaneous outpouring of billions of tonnes of lava and this, in turn, could cause the eventual structural collapse of the entire western flank of the island.'

'Interlocking vent eruptions?' said Tom, 'I'm sorry, you've lost me.'

'Cumbre Vieja isn't a volcano with just one vent or opening. It's really a line of small volcanoes with as many as twenty vents, or openings, along the ridge.'

Maria looked around the kitchen, as if searching for something, and then asked Tom if he had such a thing as a rubber glove and a pair of scissors that she could borrow.

'Sure,' said Tom, more confused than ever as he went over to a cupboard underneath the kitchen sink and fished out a bright yellow pair of gloves and a large pair of old kitchen scissors.

'Will these do?' he said, holding up the two items and looking towards Maria.

'Perfect,' she replied, taking the items from Tom's outstretched hand.

Taking one of the gloves in her right hand, she breathed into the open end and rapidly inflated it so that the fingers were erect and the palm area was bulging. Then, holding the wrist area tightly so as to prevent an escape of air, Maria began to explain.

'Imagine that the inflated palm of this glove is the batholith below the ridge.' The return of a perplexed look on Tom's face indicated to Maria that an explanation in lay man's terms was called for.

'Batholith is just another name for a large magma chamber and each inflated finger on the glove represents, in this case, one of five volcanoes arranged along the ridge above the magma chamber.'

Maria turned the glove through ninety degrees so Tom could better appreciate the linear arrangement of the volcanoes along the ridge.

Tom nodded that he understood.

'Just prior to an eruption, the magma chamber expands as it is filled with plutons of magma rising from the mantle below, forcing magma into each of the volcano's feeder pipes'. Sarah squeezed the glove tighter so as to make each finger bulge slightly more. 'When the volcano eventually begins to erupt, lava, which is the name we give to magma once it appears at the surface, is ejected from the volcano and the eruption continues until the supply of magma to that volcano from the magma chamber below begins to decline. At this point, some volcanoes actually collapse as the magma which gave them form and structure is now no longer present'.

Maria looked at Tom's face to check that he was still following her and he nodded that he was.

'Now, if just one volcano erupts, as was the case with Teneguia in the south of this island back in 1971, well, there's usually no problem and certainly no major crustal collapse. But if that eruption triggers a neighbouring volcano to erupt, and then that one triggers another volcano.....'

Tom interrupted, 'Like a domino effect.'

'Precisely,' said Maria 'and that's when we have a major problem because, as an extended fissure develops, the entire volcano literally unzips itself and allows a much greater volume of magma to escape'. Maria turned towards the professor and said, 'Professor, I'll need your assistance for the next bit of this demonstration.'

Knowing where she was going with her demonstration, the professor picked up the kitchen scissors and positioned himself at Maria's side.

Working quickly, the professor snipped off the top of each glove finger, one after the other. Immediately, each finger predictably collapsed and then, more slowly, the palm area of the glove became increasing flaccid and within seconds the entire glove had deflated and was now draped over Maria's outstretched hand.

Tom was still struggling slightly to see the significance of Maria's demonstration but then, as if someone had turned a bright light on in his brain, it all began to make sense.

'So, once all the magma has gone, the entire chamber and not just the volcanoes above it collapses'.

'Exactly!' said Maria, 'and with crust above the chamber now unsupported, the whole area begins to subside and, in the case of La Palma, slides rapidly into the sea.'

'Creating a mega-slide and mega-tsunamis,' said Tom, completing Maria's explanation for her and attempting to show that he had understood what she had been trying to explain to him.

'But why doesn't the crust just sink back into the bowels of the Earth and create a massive depression?' asked Tom.

'Excellent question,' said the professor, continuing the explanation. 'You see, señor, the situation in La Palma is made so potentially lethal by the presence of a deep fault which lies between the ridge and the coast. This means the crust will slide, under the influence of gravity, towards the sea as opposed to sinking vertically, creating, as you have so correctly stated, a mega-slide and subsequent mega-tsunami – the likes of which mankind has never seen before.'

'Sounds a bit like an Armageddon scenario,' said Tom.

The professor continued, 'Señor, the phrase Armageddon has often been used, albeit inappropriately, in the media to describe how natural events such as climate change or solar storms could spell the end of the world and the end of mankind. But, should what we have described to you actually occur, for millions of people all around the Atlantic Ocean, the phrase would be most appropriate and somewhat ironical as well.'

It was now Maria's turn to look puzzled.

'Why ironical?'

The professor smiled slightly, knowing full well that he was about to demonstrate his intellectual superiority.

'Because, my dear,' he said, 'the word Armageddon is translated from the Hebrew word -*har m giddô* - meaning a mountain ridge or range of hills, which is somewhat ironic don't you think, given our current location and what might well happen to this range of hills before too long.'

Patronising, pompous, but always infuriatingly brilliant, thought Maria, as the professor smiled and, turning away from them both, began walking towards the finca's courtyard saying, as he went,

'Now, shall we go and visit this area of discoloured trees that Señor, ...?'

'Baxter,' said Tom, 'my name is Señor Baxter.'

'Thank you,' said the professor, and then continued, 'that Señor Baxter has so helpfully told us about.'

'But there's nowhere along that part of the ridge to land your chopper,' said Tom.

'Well, in that case,' replied the Professor, 'I should be grateful if you would take us there in that splendid piece of World War 2 transport that you have parked in your courtyard.'

Delighted that anyone should consider his jeep to be 'splendid,' Tom said, 'No problem, but you should know that it's not going to be half as comfortable as your helicopter and you'd best be prepared for a bumpy ride.'

But comfort was the furthest thing from either of the two scientists' minds as they walked across the courtyard and climbed into the rear of Tom's jeep. Both were secretly extremely troubled by Tom's description of the misaligned trees and sulphurous odours and were anxious as to what they might indicate.

Once they were all seated in the jeep Tom reached to turn the ignition key into the 'on' position. As he did so, he felt a small vibration in the steering wheel. The vibration grew rapidly in intensity and soon the entire steering wheel and column began to judder and pulsate, almost as if the engine of the jeep had started – but, somewhat strangely, he hadn't, as yet, turned the key. Within a split second, the entire jeep began to shudder and then shake violently. Then, like a guard dog warning an intruder to stay away, the ground below the jeep began to emanate a low growling noise and a series of deafening cracks, like rifle shots, rang out and reverberated around the small courtyard. As the ferocity of the forces shaking the jeep intensified, tiles from the roof of the barn started to rain down on them and, with one arm raised above their heads to protect themselves from the deluge and with the other clutching at anything that would prevent them from being flung from the vehicle, the three passengers were violently tossed up and down and simultaneously backwards and forwards by a quake which was clearly of considerable magnitude.

Then the stone floor of the courtyard appeared, as if in slow motion, to be moving up and down and a crack, small at first, began to open in the ground to the left of the jeep and as the crack grew longer and wider, Tom could feel himself and the rear of the jeep being slowly lifted upwards off the floor of the courtyard.

Suddenly, as quickly as it had begun, the chaos stopped dead, and only the whimpering of Daisy could be heard in the now otherwise totally silent courtyard.

After a minute or so, Maria broke the silence, 'Are we all ok?' she asked.

Such was his state of shock, Tom was unable to answer. He tried to speak, but his words would not come. He just sat, staring into space, trying to make sense of what had just happened and was completely oblivious to the blood slowly trickling down his face from a gash in his head. Maria looked around the courtyard for the professor as he was no longer seated in the jeep. Fearing that he had been flung to the stone floor during the quake, she was relieved to see him crouching close to the edge of the crack, which now traversed the courtyard from one end to the other and disappeared under the barn. He was looking down into the chasm with his head inclined slightly to one side, and appeared to be listening to something.

'Are you ok, professor?' she called.

'Yes fine,' he replied, without looking up. 'Can you hear it, Maria?' he asked.

'Hear what?' said Maria, as she climbed unsteadily from the jeep and joined the professor by the edge of the fissure.

'Listen,' repeated the professor, with his forefinger held against his upper lip as an indication that she shouldn't speak.

Mara listened intently. Somewhere in the fissure, at an indeterminate depth, something was hissing, like an angry snake about to strike.

'I think I can hear steam,' she said to him after a moment.

'So can I.' said the professor. 'And if it is steam, we could have a major problem on our hands.'

Tom found his voice at that point and croaked almost

inaudibly, 'Look!'

The professor and Maria turned towards him and then looked in the direction that Tom's outstretched arm was pointing. In the distance, towards the far northern end of the volcanic ridge, a single dark grey column of steam and ash was billowing skywards, and as they watched, transfixed, a second and then a third column of steam and ash became visible.

'It's begun,' said the professor, 'and only God knows how it will end.'

Chapter 18

Adolfo Suárez Madrid–Barajas Airport, Spain

From the moment she had taken her seat on the plane at Gatwick Airport, Sarah had been in a state of utmost turmoil. Question after question had galloped through her mind during the first leg of her journey and now, as she waited in the departure lounge at Madrid Airport for her 2:00 p.m. connecting flight to La Palma, her confusion was as greater than ever. She was not normally an indecisive person, but on this particular matter she didn't know what to do for the best. She knew what she '*should do*' when she landed in La Palma. She '*should*' be going straight back to Tom at the farm. But whilst her head was telling her one thing, her heart was telling her something completely different and the temptation to call Carlos and ask him to meet her at La Palma airport was growing stronger by the minute.

Her mental confusion was suddenly interrupted by an announcement over the airport's tannoy that her fight to La Palma had been cancelled. As no reason was given, she went immediately to the Iberian Airways information desk where she was told about the Spanish Aviation Authority's decision to suspend all flights to La Palma until further notice owing to the ash cloud.

'Ash cloud? What ash cloud?' asked Sarah.

'From the volcano,' said the young receptionist behind the desk. 'Haven't you heard? It's all over the news.'

Sarah turned to one of the airport's numerous wall mounted TV screens which showed CNN news, twenty four hours a day. Scenes of people being herded into buses and roads packed with vehicles loaded up with personal belongings, filled the screen. Such was her confused mental state that she'd been sitting in the airport for over two hours and hadn't even glanced up at any of the screens or, if she had, it hadn't registered where in the world such chaos was happening.

'One of the volcanoes on the island has started to erupt,' the receptionist continued.

'My God', said Sarah, 'I knew there had been some quakes the other day, but I didn't know anything about an eruption. When did it start?'

'Yesterday afternoon,' replied the receptionist. 'People in the south of the island are already being evacuated and those in other parts of the island are being advised to stay indoors. Apparently, the Army has set up an exclusion zone on the ridge.'

'Which ridge?' asked Sarah, with mounting panic in her voice.

'Cumbre Vieja.' replied the receptionist.

Sarah's face paled instantaneously and she now knew what she must do. Tom was her husband and he was in danger and she had to get to him as quickly as possible.

'Is there any other way I can get to La Palma?'

'Si' said the receptionist,' 'we still have flights into Gran Canaria and I believe you can still catch a ferry from there to La Palma.'

'Ok,' said Sarah, 'I'll do that then.'

And, within three hours, Sarah was aboard the Dolphin of the Seas and heading home, to what she could not imagine, but she could only pray that all that she held dear was still safe and free from danger.

Apart from a handful of fellow travellers, she had the boat very much to herself. Normally it would have been packed with tourists en route to view La Palma's beautiful scenery and, ironically, its volcanic landscapes. But given the current situation she was amazed that there was anyone else on board at all and even the captain of the ferry had been in two minds as to whether he should set sail or not. Reports on his radio indicated that things on La Palma were getting worse by the hour and, having personally witnessed as a young man the eruption of Teneguia some forty years ago, the captain had no wish to be anywhere near an eruption, at sea or not. However, when he was told by his bosses that the quay at Santa Cruz was full of people wishing to leave the island he felt duty bound to go to their aid.

The three hour trip certainly gave Sarah plenty of time to plan what she should do next and to think about what she would say to Tom when she saw him. Although he still hadn't replied to her text, she nevertheless felt sure that he was safe and was confident that he would be there to meet her at the port. Tom had to be her top priority, but when she tried to call him and couldn't get a connection, she was left with no option but to call Carlos instead.

The news that Carlos had to impart was not good. He had not heard from Tom either and apparently the track leading up to their farm was impassable due to rock falls. Also, because of the gas emissions, the Army had made the area a no-go zone and he himself had been visited by the National Guard earlier in the day and advised to get out while he still could.

Sarah was deeply worried by what Carlos had to say.

'What can I do?' she said. 'Is there any other way we can get to the farm other than by road?'

There was a long silence and for a moment Sarah thought that she had lost her connection, until suddenly Carlos spoke.

'There's an old goat track up the eastern side of the ridge, but it is very steep and I don't know if it will be passable after the quakes.'

'We'll have to try it' said Sarah. 'I have to find out if Tom is safe. Can you meet me at the port when we dock?'

Carlos was struck by Sarah's obvious devotion to Tom and by her desire to find him, but at the same time he couldn't help feeling a fraction jealous and disappointed because it was obvious that it was Tom, and not himself, that had brought her back to the island. Clearly, he had misread the signals when she had texted him about her return.

'Of course,' said Carlos. 'I'll be waiting for you when you dock.'

Chapter 19

Granja de los Pinos, La Palma

Day 3

As Tom sat and received treatment from an army medic for the deep cut to his head that he had sustained during yesterday's quake, he silently watched the scene that was rapidly unfolding before him.

His once tranquil and peaceful farm was now a hive of activity and, still in a state of shock, he was finding it difficult to comprehend just how quickly things had happened since the quake had struck and the fissure opened up. A call on the helicopter's radio by the professor to the Director General at the Institute's headquarters in Madrid, had precipitated the arrival of a posse of geologists from all over Spain and, as news of the eruption spread around the globe, they were soon joined by earth scientists from the British Geological Survey and the USGS.

A small, but rapidly growing village of tents had sprung up at the far end of his farm, and the air literally pulsated with the sound of helicopters ferrying in either scientific equipment or yet another team of flack jacketed volcanologists. The smell of sulphur and wet steam from the recently opened fissure was now all pervading and the three erupting vents, further along the ridge, continued to belch pumice and steam higher and higher into the air. Further down the ridge, the Army was very much in evidence. They had clearly been tasked with keeping civilians away from the area and scores of machine gun totting paramilitary style personnel were now dotted all over the mountainside.

The world's media had also been quick to pick up on the fast developing situation and, after circling in their helicopters, like vultures above a distressed animal, they too had descended and were now eagerly giving a news hungry world their assessment of what was happening.

Tom, like the professor, was no lover of the media, especially as his profession had been repeatedly vilified by them during his career whenever they had taken any type of industrial action. And, although not within earshot of any of the clusters of journalists scattered around his farm or close enough to see their facial expressions, he could imagine the utterly false, grave look that each journalist would have adopted as they told their viewers about the gravity of the situation, interspersing their report with words such as apocalypse or armageddon.

Of course, to add credibility to their broadcast, more often than not an eminent scientist would be invited to join them and give the world, in a mere fifteen second slot, a supposedly detailed and accurate assessment of what *"could"* potentially happen in the next few hours.

Such was the case when the two geologists from UCL arrived on the scene and whose paper on the potential collapse of Cumbre Vieja had caused so much controversy and split the academic community some years ago. Within a few minutes of them landing, both were surrounded by a mob of microphone wielding journalists, all clambering for answers to the usual and highly predictable questions of 'When will it blow?' and 'How big will it be?'

Tom caught sight of the professor who seemed to be in a high state of excitement and very much in his element. Barking

instructions to the team of Spanish volcanologists that had been
sent to assist him, he had now donned his asbestos suit and,
with helmet under his arm, was preparing to lead an inaugural
reconnaissance mission along the ridge. An anxious Maria stood
close by, similarly dressed in protective clothing, and deep in
conversation with a young American volcanologist who had just
arrived by helicopter from Gran Canaria.

'He thinks he's the new Maurice Krafft,' said Maria to Ross,
looking towards the professor, who was now gesticulating wildly
as he spoke to the team of Spanish volcanologists.

'There's absolutely no need for us to go to the main crater
of the volcano as the telemetry gauges are giving us all the
information we need to know about the state of the magma
chamber, but he's insisting that we need to get closer, so as to
immediately assess the nature of the magma when it breaks
through.'

Ross knew that the type of magma that eventually emerged
would very much determine how this eruption was going to
proceed and was tempted to say that he believed the professor
was right, but thought better of it when he saw the concerned look
on Maria's face who was clearly terrified about what the professor
was proposing.

'I'm not sure I want to end up like the Kraffts,' said Maria.
'Burned to a crisp, or my body never ever being recovered. I know
that the professor wants to give his life, literally, to volcanicity and
enter the "Volcanologist who died in action" hall of fame, but that's
one club I am not interested in joining.'

'Problem is,' said Ross after a moment's contemplation, 'we
have no instruments in situ to assess the amount of silicon dioxide
in the magma or its temperature and viscosity. If it's relatively
cool, andesitic or rhyolitic magma, with a high gas content and
viscosity, then it could well begin to solidify in the feeder conduits

and then we could be looking at a highly explosive Vesuvian type eruption.'

'I am aware of that,' said Maria, 'but I don't think we're looking at another Mt St Helen's type eruption here. Chances are it will be a low viscosity, basaltic magma which, being less gaseous and at a higher temperature, will flow freely from the vents and not lead to a build-up of pressure and cataclysmic explosion.'

'Well,' replied Ross, 'until we get closer, we won't know what we're dealing with and I, for one, would like a heads up on this because I don't want to be hanging about on this ridge if it is andesitic or rhyolitic magma.'

'Well, perhaps you'd like to join us then, up at the crater,' said Maria sharply, her anxiety getting the better of her.

'I will be,' replied Ross. 'The USGS helicopter will be following yours; it's all been agreed already.'

Maria was relieved by Ross' revelation that he would be coming with them. It would be reassuring to have him by her side, but it would also mean that he, too, would be in great danger.

Tom was watching the pair of young scientists from what remained of the finca's courtyard with interest. They seemed to know each other and when Maria reached up and gently touched the face of the American volcanologist, it was clear that they were more than just good friends or colleagues. However, their conversation was interrupted by the professor, who had now joined them.

'We need to go,' he said. 'Now is not the time for renewing old acquaintances. We have work to do and that must be our top priority.'

And with that, he turned and walked briskly towards the waiting helicopter.

Did I detect a hint of jealously in his voice? thought Maria momentarily, and then, turning away from Ross, began walking slowly towards the helicopter too. After a few paces she paused, as if she was about to turn and face him again, but then continued on, raising her right arm in a gesture of farewell and climbed into the awaiting craft.

As Tom watched the professor and Maria's helicopter rise slowly into the air, its nose dipping slightly as it rotated into a northerly flight path, a sense of foreboding began to creep through his body and he had a strange feeling that it would be the last time that he would see the two scientists alive.

Chapter 20

The Summit of Cumbre Vieja, La Palma

Day 3

As the helicopter carrying the professor and Maria hovered over the ridge, close to the summit of Cumbre Vieja, it was immediately apparent to both scientists what they were dealing with. From the gaping fissure which ran for several miles roughly along the apex of the ridge, lava was pouring out in vast quantities and in some places, presumably vents, it was shooting hundreds of feet into the sky and spraying countless lava bombs in all directions. As dusk approached, these glowing, bright red molten missiles hissed and arched their way across the rapidly darkening sky, leaving a pale grey trail of smoke and gas in their wake. Then they could be seen falling rapidly back to earth, their bright red hue quickly fading as the air cooled the molten lava, causing it to solidify and reform into dark grey rock. Whatever they hit on landing was either smashed into a thousand pieces if the lava bomb had reformed into rock, or instantly incinerated, if it was still in a molten state.

Rapidly rising columns of steam and gas were causing their helicopter to bob violently up and down, like a small boat on a tempestuous sea, and the acrid smell of the steam filled the Perspex bubble of the cockpit as their pilot fought to hover above the inferno which raged below them.

From their elevated position, Maria could see that the lava was moving in a series of elongated flows down the western flank of the ridge. Travelling faster than a man could run, and with their surface cooled by contact with the air into a black, wrinkled, almost skin-like crust, the lava flows looked like numerous dark snakes emerging from a nest, winding and twisting their way rapidly down-slope and devouring all that stood in their path. Occasionally, where the black crust had stretched and cracked, the red molten lava within would become briefly visible and it would send a thin shaft of light upwards into the darkening sky, almost like a war time searchlight scanning the sky for enemy aircraft.

Maria, with her mouth slightly agape, stared in awe and wonder at the raw destructive forces of nature which were at work below her. Isolated pine trees on the upper most slopes of the ridge were the first to succumb to these molten ribbons of death and destruction; the precise incineration point of each tree being marked by a small flare of brilliant white light, which would then rapidly disappear as the tree was swallowed and digested by the flow. Next in line for destruction were the vineyards and isolated farmsteads on the middle slopes of the ridge and Maria watched in silent horror as, one by one, people's homes and livelihoods were ignited, incinerated and ultimately consumed. The villas of La Palma's wealthier sectors of society, which had also been built on the middle slopes of the ridge so as to afford their rich occupants an uninterrupted view of the Atlantic Ocean a few miles to the west, also succumbed, one by one, to the inexorably advancing lava flows.

But when the lava flows reached the relatively flat land of the Los Llanios Valley, their rate of advance slowed as each one began to spread out, eventually coalescing into a single, much wider flow which occupied almost the entire width of the valley bottom. Whilst the pace of destruction slowed, Maria could see that its scale was about to become much greater, because lying directly in the path of this all-consuming molten mass, were numerous villages and towns. The village of El Paso, where some of Maria's relatives lived, was the first to be devoured and those of Tacande de Ariba, Triana and Los Punos soon followed. Maria was later to learn that some villagers had tried to halt its advance by throwing buckets of water on to its leading edge, but their brave efforts to safeguard their homes and livelihoods proved futile and such attempts were quickly abandoned – as too were the houses they had been seeking to protect. Nothing, but absolutely nothing was going to stop this juggernaut of destruction until it reached its final destination of the distant Atlantic Ocean.

'It's like Dante's Inferno down there,' shouted the professor, who was struggling to make himself heard over the combined noise of the helicopter's engine and exploding lava bombs.

Maria nodded her head in agreement - too terrified by what she could see below to speak.

'From the way it's flowing freely, it very much looks like basaltic magma,' said the professor excitedly, 'but we'll know more when we land.'

'Land where?' shouted the pilot. 'I can't put down in this area; it would be suicide. As it is, I'm running the risk of being hit by a lava bomb at any second by just being this close.'

The engine of the helicopter spluttered slightly as he spoke, and then an increasingly high pitched whine could be heard coming from the rota blades above their heads. The pilot's face was contorted with panic as he shouted, 'The gas and ash are starving the engine of air and it could stall at any moment!'

'We have to land,' shouted the professor. 'I need to check the position of the fault on the ridge's western flank.'

Instantly, Maria knew why the professor was so desperate to assess this side of the ridge, as any sign of major crustal subsidence on its western flank could indicate an impending mega-slide and that could trigger a mega-tsunami.

'It's much too dangerous to land,' reiterated the pilot, who was now desperately struggling to hold the helicopter steady in the violently oscillating currents of hot gas and steam.

'There must be a way,' shouted the professor. 'I'll only need a few minutes on the ground to make my assessment and then we can take off again.'

Maria shook her head in disbelief at the professor's insistence on wanting to make what was almost certainly a suicidal landing, but her mouth was so dry with fear that she couldn't voice her objection to his proposed life threatening course of action.

'It can't be done,' replied the pilot. As he spoke, a lava bomb, hissing and whistling its way back to Earth, passed by just in front of the helicopter's cockpit.

'Jesus Christ, that one nearly hit us,' cried the pilot, his voice barely audible above the helicopter's now screaming engine.

'Look!' shouted Maria. 'Down there!' The forefinger of her asbestos gloved hand pointed to a group of three silver suited scientists who, half crawling, half crouching, were slowly making their way up the eastern flank of the ridge.

'It must be the Americans,' said the professor. 'How the hell did they get down there?'

'I don't know,' replied the pilot, 'but what I do know, sir, is that you shan't be joining them because we're getting out of here – now!'

And before the professor could protest, the pilot had banked hard to the left and began climbing rapidly above the billowing clouds of steam and gas. As he did so, Maria thought she'd caught sight of what looked like an exploding lava bomb close to where the three scientists were sheltering from the deadly deluge of red hot rock.

'What is it?' said the Professor, when he saw the look on

Maria's face.

But Maria didn't reply. She just stared ahead with a tear slowly flowing down her cheek.

Chapter 21

Villa Gaia, Los Llanios Valley, La Palma.

Franco's head was hurting, more than it had ever hurt before. The pain was so bad that he was finding it difficult to see and a feeling of nausea began to well up inside him as he shuffled in his silk dressing gown towards the bathroom to find an aspirin.

'Christ, this is one hell of a hangover,' he groaned, as his trembling hands fumbled with the child proof cap of the pill bottle. 'Fuck it!' he shouted in frustration as the cap proved too difficult for him to open and he flung the glass bottle against the white tiles of the bathroom wall.

Staggering into the lounge, he slumped into a leather reclining chair and reached for the half empty bottle of vodka that lay, on its side, on a nearby table. The cap of this bottle proved a much easier proposition for him to open and, within seconds, the bottle's neck was between his lips and he began greedily gulping down the spirit.

Kill or cure, he thought, as he pulled the bottle from his lips and wiped his mouth with the back of his hand.

Franco then took a joint from the pocket of his dressing gown, lit it and then took one long inhalation, followed by three shorter, more rapid ones. After several more pulls on the cannabis joint, Franco's headache felt no better, but the anger within him had begun to subside slightly; that was until his thoughts turned to last night's conversation with Christina. Franco's jaw visibly tensed,

making the veins in his neck stick out, as he remembered what
Christina had said to him.

'Fucking bitch!' he hissed through clenched teeth, as his anger
began to mount again and the throbbing in his temples intensified.

'Why won't she marry me? She's going to fuck everything up if
she doesn't.'

Franco's carefully laid plans of divorce from Consuela, then
a Registry Office wedding to Christina, followed by a quickie
divorce, were rapidly unravelling, following her refusal last night
to marry him.

Christina may have been desperate for male company and
Franco had certainly proved a useful distraction over the last
few months, but she was not a stupid woman, or not as stupid as
Franco thought in any event. Moreover, her investigations into
Franco's past had proved more fruitful than those previously
conducted by the Gonzales family and she had long since decided
that Franco would remain her plaything and nothing more until, of
course, she tired of him.

Franco closed his eyes and waited for the vodka and cannabis
to take effect. *A change of plan was clearly needed*, he thought. But
what exactly that would be, was proving difficult to formulate in
his hung over state.

As Franco reclined on the leather chair, the smell of burning
wood from somewhere outside the villa briefly caught his attention
but he thought little of it as the mind numbing effects of the
cannabis began to take hold. Even when gossamer thin wisps of
smoke began to drift about the floor of the villa's lounge, Franco
failed to pay any heed and remained with his eyes closed, plotting,
in spite of his thumping headache, his next move. Franco coughed
and then coughed again as more and more smoke slowly crept
through an open window and began to swirl around his feet. But
by now the vodka and the cannabis had him tightly in their grip

and were pushing him closer and closer towards the deep abyss of a drug induced stupor and he remained completely unaware of what was fast developing around him. Franco could feel himself falling deeper and deeper into a dark, soft place. It felt good, almost sexual, and he let himself succumb to it its seductive embrace totally and utterly. Memories of his childhood on the streets of Barcelona, some good, some bad, began to drift in and out of his thoughts; his first drink, his first beating at the hands of his erstwhile father and, of course, his first sexual encounter formed and then disappeared in his mind as he spiralled down and down into a semi-comatose state. Gradually his grip on the cannabis joint loosened and, as it fell from his fingers to the floor, its pungent fumes mingled with the acrid grey layer of smoke which, like an early morning mist, now lay several inches thick across the floor of the lounge.

Outside, the leading edge of the lava flow was inexorably making its way across the villa's garden, incinerating all that stood in its path. Eventually, it reached the villa's pool where, like a huge black snake, it slowly slid into the shimmering aquamarine water, hissing and spitting as it disappeared beneath the surface, instantly creating a billowing cloud of steam and gas. Within minutes the water in the pool had completely evaporated and had been replaced by a solid, rectangular, black mass of steaming hot rock, over which the next wave of lava crept slowly but easily until it reached the French doors of the lounge. The sound of cracking panes of glass and the splintering of the door's wooden frame failed to wake Franco. Seconds later the lava had made its way through where the French doors had been and began slowly and silently snaking its way across the marbled white floor of the lounge. As it coiled itself around the chair upon which Franco lay in his alcohol and drug induced state, the smell of burning leather began to mingle with that of the cannabis. Franco coughed, and then coughed again. With each inhalation his lungs were gradually filling with acrid smoke which by now had formed a dense, deep layer across the room and hung there like a grey, horizontal shroud, completely obscuring the now lava covered lounge floor and bottom half of the leather chair. Franco coughed again, but this time so violently and repeatedly that it began to drag him from his sleep. He opened one eye, and then the other. For a moment he wasn't sure if the grey murkiness of the lounge was simply the mist of a deep sleep which had yet to clear, but as the high pitched beeping of a smoke alarm somewhere in the villa began an assault on his still befuddled mind, he slowly and then rapidly began to realise that the room was full of smoke and that something, somewhere in the villa, must be on fire. Franco sat bolt upright, swung his legs from their horizontal position on the leather recliner and onto the lounge floor and then stood upright. The room swam before his eyes and he let out a high pitched, almost primeval scream as the red hot lava welded itself to the skin on the soles of his feet. Instinctively, Franco flung himself backwards onto the leather recliner and, with the excruciating pain from his badly burned feet now rapidly coursing upwards through his entire body, lay there, quivering and whimpering, like a child who had awoken from a nightmare, bewildered, terrified and wondering what to do next.

But Franco need not have concerned himself with trying to formulate an escape plan. Soon the wooden frame of the reclining chair was alight and slowly, but surely, the chair began to collapse, gradually lowering, inch by inch, the crying and simpering Franco, closer and closer towards the hissing, black surface of the lava flow.

And, before Franco's last scream of agony had rung out, the distinctive sweet smell of burning flesh had joined that of leather, cannabis and molten rock.

Chapter 22

The Port at Santa de la Cruz, La Palma

As the ferry reached La Palma, Sarah was astounded by the size of the crowd that had congregated on the quayside. People of all ages and from all walks of life were waiting there; some patiently and passively whilst others, and especially those with young children, appeared far less calm and the tension and anxiety that they were clearly feeling was etched on their faces. As the gang plank of the ferry was lowered to permit foot passengers to disembark, the crowd began to surge forward. A voice, presumably that of the ferry's captain, boomed out over the ship's loud speaker system, ordering them to get back and asking for calm, but it was hardly audible over the rising sound of crying babies and shouting parents desperate to get their children on board.

Suddenly, with the gang plank still suspended above the dock side, a metal guard rail which was positioned so as to separate people waiting to embark from the edge of the quay, gave way, and a dozen or so men, women and children spilled forward. Only the quick thinking of a dockside worker prevented a tragedy from occurring as he had the presence of mind to yank the slackened rope that he was holding into a taut position and afford the tumbling people an extra barrier to hold onto. Sarah, along with the handful of passengers who were waiting to disembark, gave a sigh of relief as the disaster was averted, but the atmosphere of panic and fear that emanated from below them was almost palpable.

Sarah tried to see if Carlos was waiting for her, but the large number of people on the quayside prevented her from doing so and it wasn't until she had disembarked and fought her way through the crush of people that she eventually found him waiting, as he had promised that he would, near the ferry company's information office.

Their meeting proved to be more awkward than she had anticipated. Sarah would have liked to have thrown herself into his powerful arms and tell him how much she had missed him, but something prevented her from doing so. He, too, wanted to embrace her, but for probably the same intangible reason as Sarah, was reluctant to do so. Instead, they both found themselves politely greeting one another with trivial questions about each other's state of well-being and such like.

The walk to Carlos' car which was parked nearby proved equally uncomfortable but, once seated inside, the atmosphere became less tense and conversation between them began to flow more freely, especially when discussion turned to that of Tom's whereabouts.

'The last time I saw him was yesterday morning,' said Carlos. 'We had breakfast together in Funacaliente and he was in good spirits.'

Sarah was pleased to learn that Tom was happy in spite of her recent departure.

'That's a relief,' she said. 'I wondered how he would react after I told him that I was leaving him.'

Carlos was tempted to play down the feelings of despair that Tom had experienced when she had first left and by doing so ingratiate himself with Sarah. However, given the circumstances, Carlos decided that it would have been both inappropriate and slightly underhand to do so, therefore he told her how Tom had spent many a night at his finca, drinking heavily after she had first left.

'And, apart from you, has he managed to find someone to comfort….'

Sarah's voice trailed away, not wishing to discover the answer to a question that had played on her mind from time to time over recent months.

Anticipating what she was loathe to ask, Carlos replied truthfully,

'No, Sarah, he hasn't. Both he and I have spent our nights together, but alone; just like two sad, middle aged men, playing cards, drinking heavily and totally bereft of female company.'

On this point Carlos was, in fact, being slightly economical with the truth as he had actually spent one night a few weeks ago in the company of the waitress who had served him in the café in Funacaliente, but this was something that Sarah didn't need to know, nor did he want her to.

Night was beginning to fall when they eventually managed to weave their way through the traffic heading towards the port and reach the road which would take them south towards Funacaliente. As they drove through numerous, dark and presumably recently evacuated villages, Carlos explained his plan and stressed that what they were about to do was fraught with difficulties and dangers.

But Sarah was not to be dissuaded. Her husband was, to all intents and purposes, missing, maybe even dead somewhere on Cumbre Vieja and she would not rest until she found him.

'Let's at least wait until first light before setting out,' said Carlos.

Sarah considered his suggestion for a minute and, as she had been travelling for nearly twenty four hours and was totally and utterly exhausted, replied,

'OK, but where are we going to stay? Both your farm and mine are in the exclusion zone so we can't stay there.'

'Don't worry,' said Carlos. 'I realised that you would need to rest after your journey and as all the hotels have closed, I've brought some sleeping bags so we can camp at the base of the ridge tonight and set off at dawn.'

Sarah was touched by his thoughtfulness and, in spite of the circumstances, was a fraction excited at the thought of spending a night under the stars with Carlos. She reached across the car and touched Carlos' arm lightly to indicate her gratitude for all that he was doing for her. And, as it lingered there for a fraction longer than normally would be the case between friends, Carlos' heart quickened slightly. *Perhaps he hadn't misread the signals after all,* he thought to himself.

Slightly embarrassed, Sarah quickly withdrew her hand, but the words that Carlos spoke next shattered the sexual tension that was building inexorably between them.

'Look to your right, Sarah.'

'Why?' she replied, with a note of puzzlement in her voice, but turned her head nevertheless to look out of the passenger window at the distant mountains.

'What can you see?'

'Just the sun setting behind the mountain tops, that all.'

'Sarah, correct me if I'm wrong, but didn't the sun set about an hour ago?'

Sarah stared at the skyline again. The tops of the mountains seemed to be edged with a thin line of bright gold and the sky immediately above several peaks was tinted blood red, almost as if a setting sun had just disappeared behind them.

'Oh my God!' exclaimed Sarah. 'Is that what I think it is?'

'I think it is. And, if I'm not mistaken, that's the glow of a much bigger eruption than I had expected and the chances of us getting to your farm and finding...'

His voiced trailed away.

'Tom alive,' said Sarah, her voice quavering with fear as she finished his sentence for him.

But before either of them could say anything more, the flashing blue lights of a police car approaching quickly from behind caught Carlos' attention and he slowed his car and then stopped.

The police car pulled up alongside them on the other side of the road and the two officers inside got out and walked towards where Carlos had stopped his car.

'Where are you heading for, señores?' said one of the policemen, as he shone the beam of his torch onto Carlos' and then Sarah's face.

'We're trying to find this lady's husband who we think is trapped somewhere up on the ridge,' said Carlos.

'I am afraid you cannot go any further in this direction,' said the younger looking of the two policemen, who now had one of his hands resting on the door frame of Carlos' car and the other on the automatic pistol that he had strapped to the belt of his trousers.

'It's far too dangerous and I should like you to turn your car around and head back towards Santa Cruz. If you hurry, you may well be in time to catch a ferry to Gran Canaria.'

'But I have to find my husband,' insisted Sarah.

Hearing the tone of desperation in her voice, the younger policeman's previously officious tone softened slightly.

'Chances are your husband has already left the island, señora. He may well have caught the last flight out of the airport before it was closed or been on a ferry for Gran Canaria.'

Sarah thought back to the congested quayside she had witnessed on her arrival but was sure that, in spite of the crowd, she would have seen Tom if he had been there.

'No, I think he's still on the island,' said Sarah to the policeman.

Shaking his head slightly, the younger policeman said,

'Be that as it may, señores, I cannot allow you to continue on this road and you must turn back for your own safety.'

From the policeman's now much sterner tone of voice it was obvious that he was no longer making a recommendation, but giving them a direct order. Carlos nodded his compliance, restarted his car and turned it back towards where they had come from and slowly drove off. Satisfied that they were obeying their instructions, the policemen returned to their vehicle and headed off at high speed in the direction of Funacaliente to the south. Carlos waited until he could no longer see the lights of the police car in his rear view mirror and then brought his car to an abrupt stop.

'What are you doing?' asked Sarah.

'I'm doing what we came here to do,' said Carlos, turning his car around once again.

'We're going south to find Tom and no 'country policeman' is going to stop us!'

A multitude of feelings washed quickly over Sarah. Relief that they were still looking for Tom, mixed with admiration for Carlos' bravery and fear of what possibly lay ahead, simultaneously coursed through her veins and made her feel slightly breathless and light headed - as did the mounting sense of excitement that she felt at being in the company of a man whom she was finding more and more attractive by the second.

In the darkness of the car's interior, Sarah reached for Carlos' arm for a second time.

'Ok, Carlos, if you're sure that's what you want to do.'

Carlos did not reply but fixed his gaze on the dark road ahead and this time Sarah left her hand resting on his muscular forearm, no longer worried about sending out the wrong signals and was secretly pleased when she saw the corners of his mouth beginning to form a smile.

Chapter 23

Hotel Playa de la Americas, Tenerife.

It was late afternoon before Consuela managed to get a break and could return to her room. The letter from Franco and who had delivered it had played on her mind throughout the day and, although she didn't want to read it and discover what he had to say, she knew that she couldn't rest until she had done so. When she reached her room she paused momentarily outside the door and, before inserting the key in the lock, listened intently for any sound coming from within. All seemed quiet so she unlocked the door, but paused again to listen before entering. Once inside, and with the door still open behind her, Consuela quickly surveyed the room, checking for anything out of the ordinary. Satisfied that all was well, she made her way to her dressing table where the letter from Franco stood propped up against a table lamp. Her hand quivered as she picked it up. Her mouth suddenly became dry and she swallowed hard as she tried to steel herself for the act of ripping open the envelope. But before she could do so, the mobile phone in her pocket began to vibrate, indicating an incoming call. Consuela quickly replaced the letter and reached instead for her phone. The number flashing on the screen was not one that she recognised and normally she would not have answered it. But as any delay in opening Franco's letter was a welcome one, she let it vibrate for a moment longer and then pressed the accept key. Placing the phone to her ear she gave her name and immediately the phone went dead.

'Probably a wrong number,' she mumbled to herself and was about to replace the phone in her pocket when it began to vibrate again. Consuela looked at the phone's screen and saw that it was the same number as before. When she answered it for a second time the caller didn't hang up this time, but neither did they say anything, although she could tell from what sounded like rasping, slightly laboured breathing that the caller was probably a man and he sounded like a heavy smoker.

'Pervert!' she spat with all the venom in her voice that she could muster and was about to hang up when the caller suddenly spoke.

'Did you get your letter, Señora Hernandez.?'

Consuela's heart missed a beat. The caller had used her married name, which, apart from Adrienne, nobody else on Tenerife knew.

'Señor Hernandez would like to know what your answer is and he wants to know now!' said the voice on the other end of the line.

'Who is this?' she demanded, trying not to let the fear in her voice be detected.

'Who I am is not important, but an answer to my employer's question is, and, shall we say, I am here to ensure that your answer is the one that he wishes to hear.'

The menacing tone in the man's voice was unmistakable and, as a wave of fear induced nausea swept over her, she was forced to lean against the dressing table for support.

'I don't know what you're talking about,' said Consuela. 'What answer?'

'Tut, tut, Señora Hernandez.' said the man, mockingly. 'So you haven't read the letter yet. In that case I suggest that you do so immediately and call me back with your answer on this number in five minutes' time, or else I shall be forced to visit you in person!'

The line went dead and Consuela's whole body began to tremble uncontrollably and her knees felt like they were going to give way at any second. It had been some while since she had felt such a paralysing fear and the menace in the caller's voice brought memories of the brutality that she had suffered at the hands of Franco flooding back.

Consuela picked up the letter again and was on the verge of tearing it open when a small voice in her head suddenly shouted, 'No! Don't you dare open it. He's controlled you for long enough.' And for the first time in a long while, she listened to the angels in her mind and ignored the demons and stuffed the unopened letter in her handbag, ready to take it to the police.

In the hotel car park Jose Batista pressed the off button on his phone, slipped it back into the secret compartment that he had made under the driver's seat of his car, lit another cigarette and waited patiently for Consuela to emerge from the hotel's entrance. He knew from past experience that a threatening phone call, especially to a vulnerable and frightened female, would always have the desired effect of flushing them out into the open. He allowed himself a small congratulatory smile as he recalled how easy it had been to track her down to Tenerife and to find her mobile phone number. Before being dishonourably discharged from the police force for gross professional misconduct, he had acquired many skills which were now proving most useful in his current line of work. But, most important of all, were the contacts that he had made whilst working as a police officer; contacts who, for one reason or another, were now in his debt. An employee of a local airline was one such contact and she had proved extremely helpful in finding out where Consuela had fled to some six months earlier, as too was the shop owner who had sold Consuela her mobile phone. Both owed Batista favours, but for completely different reasons. The airport employee had been arrested by the police for selling counterfeit perfumes, but thanks to Batista, the CCTV footage of her hiding the fake items in her locker at work had strangely disappeared and since then she had been only too willing to provide him with flight details of a number of people he was tracking. Likewise, the owner of the mobile phone shop had several skeletons in his cupboard relating to credit card payments to a paedophile website which Batista exploited to his advantage whenever he needed to trace a phone or hack into someone else's.

Tracking her down to the hotel where she worked had not been so easy, however, owing to his lack of contacts on Tenerife, but after trawling numerous bars and clubs with a picture of her that Franco had given him, he eventually got the break he was looking for.

Whilst waiting for her to emerge, Batista had tried to call Franco several times on his mobile to let him know that he had delivered the letter and was now going to apply the persuasive pressure that Franco had made abundantly clear should be used, if Consuela proved in any way difficult. But for some unexplained reason, each time he had rung, he had got the continuous tone, indicating a wrong number. Batista was puzzled by this and had called the number several times to make sure that he was actually calling the right one. Dismissing it as a fault of the phone company, Batista set about preparing himself for the next phase of his task. From the glove compartment of his car he took out a pair of flesh coloured latex gloves, a roll of gaffer tape and some plastic garden ties and a small container of talcum powder. Placing the tape and ties temporarily on the passenger seat, he sprinkled some talc carefully into each glove, replaced the talc, tape and ties into the glove compartment and then put on the gloves. He knew from his time in the police force that wearing the gloves for an extended period of time could result in his hands sweating excessively and he didn't want anything to affect his grip on the steering wheel of his car. Or, more importantly, on Consuela's neck. Preparations complete, Batista lit another cigarette and waited for Consuela to appear.

As expected, he didn't have long to wait before he saw Consuela emerge from the hotel's entrance and make her way to where her car was parked. He waited for her to start her car and drive past him, before putting his car into gear and then slowly followed her out onto the main road into Puerto de la Brava.

Batista had considered confronting her in the hotel car park, but that would have been too public and too easy; especially as he enjoyed his work and found stalking a prey and then terrorising them exciting and even sexually arousing. Besides, even though he had no idea where she was heading, he knew that at some point she would stop and he would then be able to make his move.

But what Batista had not considered as he tailed Consuela's car was just how congested the streets of Puerto de la Brava are in the height of the tourist season and that, on this particular weekend, the town was hosting the festivals of La Embarcacion de la Virgen del Carmen and La Sardina. Both festivals attract people from all over the island and this afternoon the streets were packed with thousands of people awaiting the climax of the La Sardina festival. Batista had never been a fan of festivals and considered the Spanish obsession with them antiquated and demeaning to Spain. He snorted out loud as he thought about how, in today's festival, a large papier mache sardine would be carried through the streets by men in drag, brought to the waterfront, "blessed" with "holy water" and then set alight, all to the rapturous applause and cheering of the on looking crowds.

'How fucking ridiculous!' muttered Batista under his breath. 'How the fuck can burning a paper fish ensure the safety of the fishing fleet and a good catch of sardines in the coming year!?'

'Fucking people!' spat Batista, as a group of festival revellers wandered along in the middle of the road, causing him to momentarily lose sight of Consuela's car. Batista sounded his horn to tell the group to move out of the way, but they simply responded by producing their own air horns and began blasting them in unison with his.

'Get out the fuckin' way!' screamed Batista, but the revellers took no notice and began a conga dance in front of his car and beckoned passers-by to join in the fun.

With his frustration mounting to fever point, Batista was on the verge of driving into them, but caught sight of a policeman sitting on his motorbike on the street corner, and decided against it. After a minute or two, however, the revellers tired of the fun they were having at Batista's expense and disappeared up a side street, blasting their air horns as they went, leaving Batista free to continue his pursuit of Consuela.

Up ahead, at the next set of traffic lights, Batista could just about see the rear of Consuela's car.

'Got her,' he snarled, and completely ignoring the police motor cyclist, drove at speed through the throng of pedestrians until he had drawn level with her at the traffic lights.

Time to introduce myself, he thought.

As she sat at the traffic lights waiting for them to turn green, Consuela glanced to her right and noticed that the man in the car next to hers was looking straight at her, and, from the movement of his lips, seemed to be saying something directly to her. Instinctively, she turned away as it was not uncommon for middle aged men on the island to mouth obscene sexual offers at lone female drivers when stationary at traffic lights. Being young and attractive, this had happened to her a number of times in the past and she had always found that looking straight ahead was always the best course of action to take. But for some inexplicable reason on this occasion she felt compelled to turn her head back towards him, and almost immediately realised that he was actually asking her a question about something of an entirely non sexual nature. She looked closely at his thick lips, which the man was moving deliberately and slowly so as to ensure that she understood what he was saying. Consuela's heart rate quickened when she realised that he seemed to be referring to her by her married name and then froze with fear as the man began to mime opening a letter and seemed to be asking her if she had read it. In an instant she realised that this was the man who must have asked Diego to deliver the letter to her room and who had just phoned her. Feelings of blind panic began to grip her entire body and, as adrenalin flooded into her nervous system, she pressed her foot hard on the accelerator pedal and drove off at speed without even looking to see if the lights had turned green. Glancing in her rear view mirror, she could see the man's car had also raced away from the lights and was now closing on hers, fast. Up ahead, the next set of lights were flashing amber and she prayed that they were about to turn green so that she could continue her escape, but when they turned red, she was forced to break hard and stop. Consuela looked to her right and a fraction of a second later the man's car screeched to a halt next to hers. The lights turned green and she set off again at high speed, but the man remained close behind her, repeatedly flashing his lights. Straight ahead, on the left hand side of the road, Consuela could see the entrance to a multi-storey car park and in her blind panic turned into it, desperately hoping that she could find somewhere to hide amongst the hundreds of cars parked inside. But Batista had anticipated what she was about to do and turned hard left as well and within seconds was behind her, on the ramp, leading up to the first level of the car park. At the top of the ramp a red and white plastic barrier was barring her way and Consuela desperately hoped that it would elevate as she approached. But as she got closer to the barrier it remained in the horizontal position and with it blocking her way forward and with Batista's car right behind hers, Consuela was trapped. Her heart was pounding, her breathing was coming in short, shallow gasps, and she knew immediately that she had made a major mistake by turning into the multi-storey car park. Then, in her rear view mirror, she saw that Batista was getting out of his car. With her hand trembling like a leaf in the wind, Consuela reached across the passenger seat of her car, towards the door lock button, but as she did so, the seatbelt went into the lock position, preventing her from reaching it. Her quivering fingers fumbled with the release mechanism of the seatbelt for what seemed like an eternity and eventually the belt went slack. But, just as her finger-tip touched the small black button of the door lock, Batista flung open her car door. Consuela tried to scream, but nothing came out and, in the next instant, he was sitting next to her. Batista was sweating profusely and the stale smell of his body odour rapidly filled the car. He grabbed her right arm roughly and yanked it towards him.

'I asked you a question, señora, and your husband would like your answer,' he snarled through his clenched, cigarette stained teeth and contorted lips.

They say that every dog has its day, and this was to be Consuela's day, for, although terrified, at that precise moment in time something in her snapped. Maybe it was the years of mistreatment at the hands of Franco, or maybe it was just her blind terror, but whatever it was, for the first time in her life, Consuela found the courage to fight back. With her free hand, she seized a metal ball point pen from the dashboard of her car and with a swift downwards movement plunged it into Batista's thigh. After the initial, fleeting resistance afforded by the thick cotton of Batista's trousers, the pen sank, like a red hot poker being thrust into wax, easily and deeply into his fleshy white thigh. Batista gasped in agony and instantly released his grip on her wrist. With both hands now free, Consuela was able to intensify her attack. She grabbed a handful of Batista's greasy black hair near his temple with her left hand and simultaneously, but inadvertently, thrust her long, manicured thumbnail into his eyeball; Consuela then used her other hand to pull the pen from his thigh and began to lunge at Batista's head with it. Partially blinded, Batista raised both arms to protect his face and uninjured eye from the relentless and frenzied onslaught, but the pen's point still managed to repeatedly puncture the skin on his forearms and forehead. Such was the ferocity of the attack that Batista was forced to turn his body away from hers and, in an effort to escape, tried to open the car door. But Consuela did not stop. Now holding the pen with both hands, and with every ounce of strength that she could muster, she continued stabbing the pen's point into Batista's back and the nape of his neck with such force that the metal shaft of the pen began to buckle and bend in her clenched fists. With the door now partially open, Batista fell from the car onto the road, where he lay, clutching the side of his neck, with blood oozing from between his fingers and groaning loudly.

Suddenly Consuela found her voice and years of fear and frustration spilled out of every pore of her being.

'You bastard, you fucking bastard!' she screamed at the top of her voice.

She looked down at the man who was now curled into a foetal position on the road and was moaning softly. For a split second, she imagined that it was Franco lying there, in a rapidly growing pool of blood. But as the adrenalin pumping through her veins began to subside, and realising that the groaning figure was not that of her husband, she suddenly started to panic about what she had just done. A feeling of nausea began to well up inside her and with her whole body shaking uncontrollably, she rammed her foot down hard on the accelerator and drove through the plastic barrier, narrowly missing an elderly car park attendant. With her blood smeared hands tightly gripping the steering wheel, and with her car tyres squealing like an animal in distress, she raced past a line of parked cars and then on to an exit ramp, before descending rapidly back to the ground floor and out onto the main road.

She did not know where she was going, or even care for that matter, and in her panicked state of mind, she didn't even notice the flashing blue lights and sirens of the police cars that were rapidly converging on the car park where Batista lay bleeding. She just had to get to somewhere safe and, without realising it, she was soon heading out of town on a road that led to the highest point on the island - a destination which, unbeknown to Consuela, would ultimately save her life

Chapter 24

Granja de los Pinos, La Palma

Day 4

As Maria and Tom stood on a small ridge behind the shattered remains of his home, looking north towards the summit of Cumbre Vieja, there were tentative signs that the eruption may well have peaked. After three days of incessant and violent activity, the three vents that had opened when the eruption started, had begun to show signs of decreasing ash and gas emissions and, mercifully, increasingly fewer explosive volleys of lava bombs were now occurring. And, although the out pouring of lava from the fissure along the ridge had yet to lessen significantly, some, but not all, of the assembled volcanologists had begun to sense that an end was perhaps in sight and the nightmare scenario of a major collapse may well have been averted.

With a lessening in the ejection of lava bombs, a Spanish Army helicopter crew had set off just after daybreak to recover the bodies of the three American volcanologists together with that of their helicopter pilot.

What they found on the eastern flank of the ridge was, predictably enough, not particularly pleasant and certainly not for Maria's eyes. Despite finding a rock outcrop to shelter under, the intensity of the deluge of lava bombs that had rained down upon the volcanologists and their pilot made formal identification of the four men virtually impossible and it was only the insignias on the tattered fragments of clothing that somehow still clung to their battered and charred bodies that ultimately permitted any kind of recognition. Ross' body had been particularly badly disfigured by what must have been a direct hit by a lava bomb, and it would be several weeks before dental records and DNA tests had confirmed his identity and the burial of his remains could take place back in his hometown of Seattle.

The slight hiatus in the eruption also provided the professor with the opportunity to attempt another landing on the volcano's summit in order to assess the degree of crustal subsidence, along with the chemical composition of the lava. He did not share the optimistic view of some of his more junior and less experienced colleagues that the worse may be over, and knew that if the lava kept coming at its present rate, then there was a strong possibility that the magma chamber would collapse along with the crust above it, triggering the nightmare scenario of a mega-slide and subsequent mega-tsunami. However, he was also sure that if the fault hadn't already slipped, and the lava flow decreased, then it was likely that a collapse would not occur.

As he climbed into the helicopter which would take him to the summit there was, however, one thing still bothering him. Why had the fissure eruption and vent opening been confined to just the northern section of the ridge? Recent eruptions on the ridge, such as that of Teneguia in 1971, had been focused in the south, near Funacaliente and he was sure that magma was rising in the southern section too because of the recent wave of seismic activity and sulphurous odours in that area. But, somewhat puzzlingly, as yet no fissure or vent had opened near to Funacaliente. There was, of course, only one possible explanation for this situation. But at this point in time the professor decided that it would be prudent to keep it to himself because, if his theory proved correct, then the scale of the current eruption would pale into insignificance compared to what might happen next.

####

'Where's the professor?' asked Tom.

'He's gone back up there,' said Maria, pointing to the upper most part of the ridge.

'The man must be insane said Tom, shaking his head in disbelief. 'You only just escaped with your lives on your last attempt. Won't he ever learn?'

'I'm afraid not,' replied Maria. 'He will not rest until he finds out if the fault has slipped and he doesn't care if he dies doing it.' As she spoke, Maria's thoughts turned momentarily to the fateful words spoken by Maurice Krafft the day before his death. Tom was on the verge of mentioning those that had already died in the name of Volcanology just the other day, but remembering the conversation he had witnessed Maria having with one of the three volcanologists who had died, fell silent and just shook his head again.

'I knew one of them, you know. One of the American scientists that died, that is.' said Maria.

Deciding to feign ignorance of the relationship that he suspected existed between them, Tom replied.

'Did you? Which one?'

'The tall, handsome one, whom you saw me talking with just before we took off in our helicopter. We were friends, very good friends, if you know what I mean, but I suspect that you had already worked that one out.'

Tom recalled the tender exchange that he had witnessed between Maria and Ross earlier and, feeling slightly embarrassed at having had his pretence exposed, said nothing, but slowly nodded his head to indicate that she was correct in her assumption.

'Where did you meet him?' asked Tom, after a short silence.

'Last year, in Hawaii. I was there on a secondment at the Mau Lau Observatory and he was on vacation there.'

'Bit of a bus man's holiday for him then,' said Tom in an attempt to lighten the tone of their conversation.

A puzzled look came over Maria's face and instantly Tom wished that he hadn't said anything.

'Oh, it's just an English expression,' he continued, but, feeling too embarrassed to complete his explanation, decided to try and change the subject. 'If the professor discovers that the fault has slipped, what will you do next?'

'There's only one thing we can do,' said Maria, 'We get the hell out of here as quickly as we can.'

'And if it hasn't slipped?'

'Well, at the current rate that magma is issuing from the chamber, if the crust hasn't already begun to collapse, then it's likely to sooner rather than later.'

'But what if the lava flows stop?'

For the first time in four days Maria smiled slightly and, pointing to the sky said, 'Then we thank the Lord for saving us, but still get the hell out of here because I suspect that Cumbre Vieja still has at least one more trick up her sleeve and it's a particularly nasty one at that .'

Tom was both perplexed and worried by Maria's comment and was about to ask her what she meant by it, when the sound of an approaching helicopter caught their attention.

'It's the professor,' said Maria, who was clearly relieved that he had managed to return safely to the farm.

As the helicopter carrying the professor touched gently down, Maria and Tom began walking towards it, both hoping that he had some good news to tell them.

As the professor climbed out of the helicopter, a small cheer went up from some members of the waiting media, causing a slight smile to form at the corners of the professor's mouth. Memories of his days with the Kraffts came momentarily flooding back as he recalled the intense media attention that always surrounded the couple whenever they held a press conference to report their findings. *Maurice and Katia would be proud of him*, he thought, as he climbed onto a rock and turned to address the waiting journalists.

The first part of the professor's report was aimed largely at the posse of journalists who were hungry for any news, good or bad. As the professor told the journalists that he could find no evidence of slippage on or near the fault, and that a mega-slide was at present unlikely to happen, Tom watched the faces of the media personnel with interest. Some, as Tom had suspected, were clearly disappointed that they would not be broadcasting a story of an impending apocalypse whilst others, presumably from more reputable newspapers and television stations, seemed genuinely relieved that their announcement to the waiting world would contain a ray of hope.

The second part of the Professor's report was not, however, for public consumption. When the media scrum had dispersed, the Professor walked over to where Maria and Tom were standing and what he had to say was not a million miles from a worrying thought that had been slowly forming in Maria's mind over the last day or so.

'There has been no discernible movement of the fault,' he began to tell them, 'and analysis of the lava reveals that its chemical composition and temperature are changing in a way that suggests that its expulsion rate has peaked and it will soon begin to slow.'

'That's great news!' exclaimed Tom.

Not for the first time since they had met, the professor chose to ignore Tom's interruption and continued. 'But I suspect there's an issue on the southernmost section of the ridge, which is a cause for major concern.'

'The failure of any vents or fissures to open around Funacaliente,' interrupted Maria.

'Precisely,' said the professor, smiling at his colleague, *who had clearly benefitted and grown intellectually under his stewardship,* he thought to himself.

'And why do you think that might be so?' said the professor.

Maria paused before giving him the answer that neither scientist truly wanted to believe was the case.

'Because,' said Maria, 'the magma under the volcano at Funacaliente is not basaltic, but probably andesitic or rhyolitic.'

Tom's mind raced back in time to the conversation that he had had with the two scientists in his kitchen about the properties of magma, which now seemed like an eternity ago.

'It's not erupting because it's viscous magma and its solidified in the vents,' Tom blurted out, excitedly.

For once, the professor's reaction to one of Tom's untimely outbursts was not one of mild annoyance or indifference. Instead, he smiled at Tom and said,

'My word, you have learned a great deal over the last few days and, for once, you are totally and utterly correct, Señor Baxter.'

'Now tell me', he continued, 'why is that a matter of concern?'

Buoyed by the professor's unusually favourable reaction to one of his comments, Tom felt sufficiently confident to repeat the analogy of a shaken champagne bottle and cork that Maria had used whilst seated around his kitchen table.

'Excellent,' said the professor, 'the magma below Teneguia may well have solidified into a plug in the main vent of the volcano and that plug may well be preventing an eruption and, just like a shaken champagne bottle, the pressure in the magma chamber below could be mounting to near bursting point. But tell me, Señor Baxter, what signs on the surface would indicate that what you have described has, in fact, happened and we are now dealing with an impending cataclysmic eruption, the size of which could possibly be similar to the Mt St Helen's eruption?'

The professor posed this question, knowing full well that Tom was not au fait with this eruption, or any eruption for that matter.

Tom shrugged his shoulders.

'A cryptodome, Señor Baxter, we would expect to see a cryptodome.'

None the wiser, Tom looked at Maria, who obliged with a brief explanation of how one side of the volcano would looked inflated.

'And that is why,' said the professor, 'we are going to Teneguia immediately to see if such a bulge has developed.'

'But won't that be a fraction dangerous,' said Tom, who for the first time began to experience the feelings of trepidation that Maria consistently did whenever the professor made one of his suggestions.

'It may well be,' replied the professor, with a glint of excitement in his eyes, 'but what is life without a little danger?'

And with that the professor began striding towards the waiting helicopter, turning as he did to summon Maria and Tom to join him

'Welcome to the world of volcanology,' said Maria to Tom, as they climbed into the helicopter and took their seat behind the professor's.

Tom's suddenly ashen face was clear indication to Maria that this was not a trip that he, nor herself, for that matter, truly wanted to make, but the professor had spoken and neither of them felt sufficiently brave at this point to refuse his invitation.

Chapter 25

United States Geological Survey, Virginia, USA

The news that the eruption of Cumbre Vieja was showing some signs of abating was received with little or no celebration by the residents of the US east coast - essentially because Professor Stevens had used his power to impose a news blackout and, until he had given orders for it to be lifted, they had had no knowledge that the eruption had been happening or of the potential peril they had been in.

Professor Stevens, however, reacted somewhat differently to the news when he heard it. To say he was relieved would have been an understatement and, although he was saddened by the loss of three of the USGS' most talented and promising young volcanologists and their pilot, he could not help feeling a sense of relief. His decision to wait and see had proved correct and, by doing so, he now felt sure that his position as Director General was probably secure, at least until his scheduled retirement next year. There was, of course, the matter of the four fatalities to explain, but given the nature and risks involved in volcanology, deaths were not unheard of and would not, he envisaged, cause too much of a media stir.

Unfortunately, the media did not see the death of the three young scientists and pilot as, to quote the professor, ' regrettable but unavoidable', and, in the weeks that followed his decision to effectively send them to their deaths, was scrutinised in the

minutest detail by all sectors of the US media. Nor did they agree
with his decision to keep everyone in the dark about what was
happening on La Palma and it was his failure to inform the US
population of just how perilous their situation had been, and his
decision not to issue any kind of alert, which was soon the focus of
media attention and would ultimately cost him his job.

It was in fact Ross' hometown newspaper, the Seattle
Chronicle, which set the media ball rolling against the professor.
An article written by an old school friend of Ross', Dexter Cole,
posed a number of questions about the circumstances surrounding
the young volcanologist's death which were subsequently picked
up by the nation's tabloid papers. Within a very short period of
time, articles likening the professor to Nero fiddling whilst Rome
burned and computer generated images of flooded east coast
cities and drowned highways were soon on all of their front pages.
The treatment that he received from more reputable papers,
although less brutal, was nonetheless equally critical. But it was
the attention and position adopted by several of the nation's TV
stations which made life particularly difficult for Professor Stevens
and which played a major part in his fall from grace and power.

One chat show host was especially vocal in her criticism of
him. Her name was Stella Davidson and she was also the daughter
of the late volcanologist, Dr John Davidson, who had died during
the eruption of Mt St Helens. Just like Ross and his colleagues,
Dr Davidson had been sent by Professor Stevens to monitor the
volcano from the observatory which lay seven miles from Mount
St Helens and it was his increasingly worrying reports about the
volcano's changing shape that had prompted Professor Stevens to
issue the evacuation order. But no such order was ever given to Dr
Davidson and he had remained at his post, totally oblivious to the
major evacuation taking place all around him, until he was hit by
the pyroclastic flow which devastated so much of the area. Stella

had never mentioned to anyone that she held Professor Stevens personally responsible for her father's death, but with the media targeting him on an almost daily basis, she seized her opportunity for revenge and, when he was invited to appear on her prime time TV programme, she very subtlety, but nonetheless decisively, drew the entire nation's attention to his deficiencies as a decision maker and effectively put the final nail in his professional coffin.

With his reputation in tatters and the media witch hunt against him showing no sign of diminishing, the professor's position as Director General of the USGS became increasingly untenable and so it came as no surprise to him when he received a phone call from the President of the US, suggesting that he should tender his resignation. A suggestion which Professor Stevens had no option but to act on and within the week his name had been removed from the USGS website and his career was over.

Chapter 26

Puerto de la Brava, Tenerife

Detective Chief Inspector Diego Martinez of Tenerife's division
of the Policia Nacional, and his colleague, Police Constable David
Gomez, looked on as the semi-conscious body of Batista was lifted
slowly and gently into the waiting ambulance.

'Will he make it?' asked the DCI in a disinterested tone of
voice that suggested that this was not the first time that he had
witnessed a crime of this type.

Constable Gomez shrugged his shoulders and said,

'The medics said that he's lost a lot of blood but should pull
through. Luckily, the attacker just missed the victim's cerotic
artery, otherwise we'd have a murder case on our hands.'

'Well, that's something, I suppose,' said the DCI, 'otherwise I'd
be cancelling all leave and that includes yours too, amigo.'

Constable Gomez inwardly breathed a sigh of relief as he was
soon to go on holiday with a woman he'd recently met and who
worked at one of the town's seafront hotels.

'Any witnesses?' asked the DCI.

'Yes, just the one though. An elderly car park attendant saw
the whole thing. Apparently, the attacker was a woman. Her car
was in front of the victim's and she set about him when he got into
her car. Sounds like a severe, but nevertheless straight forward
domestic to me. What do you think?'

The DCI's brow furrowed slightly,

'Maybe, but what the hell had he done to warrant an assault of that ferocity?'

'Had an affair perhaps? Perhaps he'd slept with her sister, or better still, her mother.'

'You know, Gomez, I sometimes worry about how that weird mind of yours works.'

'Sorry boss, just using my imagination, like you're always telling me to do.'

But the DCI was no longer listening as his attention was now firmly focused on the pool of congealed blood on the road where the man's body had lain. Noticing the bent and buckled silver coloured metal pen next to it, he took a handkerchief from his trouser pocket and stooped down to pick it up.

'I'm not so sure about this being a domestic,' he said, as he carefully inspected the blood smeared pen that he was now holding between his forefinger and thumb.

'You say the attacker was a woman and our male victim got into her car?'

'According to the car park attendant, that's what happened.'

The DCI thought for a moment before saying,

'You know, I'm not sure if our victim is a totally innocent party in all of this. It looks to me like he was actually pursuing our mystery woman and when she couldn't escape because of the barrier, he got out of his car and then into hers. What he planned to do next, I have no idea; it's too public a place for rape or a sexual assault, so maybe this was a robbery or a failed kidnap attempt, but whatever he was intending to do, or tried to do, it certainly terrified the woman and caused her to launch a very vicious attack on him.'

'So,' said Gomez, 'if she was being pursued, why didn't she lock her car doors and call for help when he trapped her at the top of the ramp?'

'Probably didn't have time.'

'Or, perhaps, she knew the man.'

'That's equally possible, but I suspect not. No, I don't think the woman knew the man, nor do I think that she expected this attack, which rules out your domestic violence theory. But I do believe that she was actually in fear of her life and this is most likely to have been an attempted robbery or probably kidnapping.'

'What makes you so sure?'

'Because,' replied the DCI, 'why would our victim have had these in his car?' The DCI pointed to the garden ties and gaffer tape in the glove compartment of Batista's car.

'Not everyday motoring items, are they? Plus, if the woman was expecting to be violently attacked by her aggrieved boyfriend or husband, surely she would have been better prepared and perhaps armed herself with a more suitable weapon such as a knife rather than a pen. No, I think he got into her car, attacked her, and in order to defend herself, she grabbed the first thing that she could lay her hands on, which in this case was a pen, probably from the dashboard of her car. Then she panicked and fled from the scene, leaving behind the pen with the name of the hotel where possibly she is either staying or employed.'

The DCI held the pen in front of his colleague's face so that he could see the name of the hotel which, although partly covered in congealed blood, was just about discernible.

When Constable Gomez saw the name of the hotel on the pen, his heart skipped a beat as it was the same hotel where the new woman in his life worked, but he chose not to mention this to his superior as it was probably just a coincidence.

'Did the victim have any ID on him?' asked the DCI.

'No, nothing at all.'

'That's suspicious in itself. No wallet, no passport?'

'No, not a thing, but we've got both of his mobile phones and should be able to identify him through that.'

'Two mobiles, you say.'

'Yes, one's a cheap pay as you go phone which we found hidden under the seat of his car, whilst the other one was in his trouser pocket and looks like a more expensive contract job.'

'I'm always suspicious if someone's got a second, pay as you go phone, aren't you?'

'No, not really. I always have a spare in my car in case the battery on my other phone runs out.'

'But you wouldn't hide it away under your car seat, would you? No, it suggests to me that he was trying to cover his tracks. I think we need to check the records of both phones to see who our mystery man is and who he has been in contact with. And, as you clearly didn't notice, I'd also like you to go to the hospital and retrieve the pink latex gloves that our mystery man was wearing when they put him in the ambulance.'

'Latex gloves. What latex gloves?' asked the constable, with a puzzled look on his face.

'Exactly', said the DCI, and then added, 'and that's why you're a constable, and I'm a DCI'

'Point taken,' said Gomez, 'Leave it with me, Boss. I'll get straight on to it.'

####

'This is interesting.' said Constable Gomez.

'What is?' asked the DCI, looking up from a document that he was reading at his office desk.

'It turns out the number plates on our victim's car were false, but I've just had the phone records of his mobiles back from the lab, and it turns out he is called Batista, and is from La Palma, where he runs a detective agency.'

'And why should that be of any interest to us?'

'Well, I thought the name rang a bell so I did some additional checking and it seems that he once was one of us, but was thrown out of the force for professional misconduct. But, more interestingly, it seems that he had some kind of business relationship going on with a pretty heavy criminal, cum restaurant owner, on La Palma.'

At the mention of a criminal connection, the DCI suddenly became more interested in the case and, sitting forward in his chair, asked,

'How do you know that?'

'Well, on the day he was attacked, he had tried to ring a particular number fifteen times and I've had the number checked and it belongs, or should I say, belonged, to an individual called Franco Hernandez who, according to police records, had a form sheet as long as your arm. Robbery, burglary, drug pushing, ABH, GBH, pimping; you name it, he'd done it.'

'Why past tense?'

'Well, Señor Hernandez is currently missing, presumed dead, after the eruption of Cumbre Vieja on La Palma. Apparently he was shacked up with some heiress in her villa in the Los Llanios Valley when it was destroyed by a lava flow. They haven't found his body and it's unlikely that they ever will, but the heiress reckons he was in there and at the precise time that the lava flow engulfed it. Plus, he hasn't turned up at the restaurant he owned, so it's increasingly looking like he's no longer with us.'

'So', said the DCI, after several minutes of deliberation, 'What have we got? Firstly, our now not so mysterious victim was possibly in the employ of a criminal and is called Batista. Secondly, Señor Hernandez is now probably dead, which means the only person who can tell us why Batista is here, on Tenerife, and where our missing woman comes into all of this, is Batista himself. But, given that he may not make it, and even if he does, will no doubt claim that he was just an innocent bystander, it is now imperative that we find our mystery female.'

Constable Gomez nodded in agreement, but paled visibly when the DCI suddenly stood up and announced that they were off to the Hotel de la Playa- the very hotel where his new girlfriend, Consuela, worked and from whom he hadn't heard a thing for nearly a day.

Chapter 27

Funacaliente, La Palma

Day 5

'I don't think we're going to find him here, Sarah,' said Carlos, as they drove through the now largely deserted streets of Funacaliente. 'Maybe that policeman was right after all, and he has left the island already,' he continued, trying to disguise the fact that secretly he hoped that was indeed the case.

As Carlos turned into the town's plaza his car was brought to a sudden and violent halt, causing Sarah and himself to be flung forward in their seats. He tried to move the car forward, but it would not budge and sound of the engine revving furiously was soon accompanied by that of metal grating on stone. Carlos got out of the car to find out what was causing the problem and was amazed to see that an elongated section of the plaza's cobbled surface had risen up into a terrace, some six inches or so higher than the surrounding cobbles, and against which the car was now lodged. Carlos looked to his right, and then left, and noted that the raised area seemed to extend from one side of the plaza to the other, and that the unmistakable smell of rotten eggs seemed to fill the air directly above it. But as he assessed the damage that his car had sustained, Carlos noticed Pedro, sitting alone, outside a closed up café on the other side of the plaza.

'Hola,' called Carlos, when he saw his elderly friend.

Pedro either didn't hear the greeting or chose to ignore it. He didn't look up, but remained with his eyes firmly fixed on the cobbles of the plaza, clutching an empty bottle of wine in one hand and the burnt out stub of a cigarette in the other. Nor did he acknowledge Carlos and Sarah's presence when, after walking across the plaza, they sat down next to the old man.

Pedro was mumbling to himself in the local dialect which Sarah, like Tom, had never been able to comprehend, even when spoken slowly, as was the case now.

'He says that this is end,' Carlos interpreted. 'He can feel it in his bones and soon Funacaliente, his birth place and home for eighty years, will no longer be here.' A strong smell of alcohol emanated from Pedro as he continued muttering to himself.

'He's completely legless,' said Sarah, in a slightly less than sympathetic tone.

'Maybe,' said Carlos, 'but this is not how Pedro normally behaves when he's the worse for wear. Aggressive, argumentative and, on the odd occasion, downright violent, yes, but never morose and melancholy like this.'

Pedro continued to mutter something which even Carlos struggled to comprehend and then, rising to a standing position, he pointed to the centre of the plaza, before limping off and then disappearing down a small alley.

But before they could look to see what he was pointing at, the sound of a helicopter approaching from behind them captured their attention. When directly overhead, the helicopter hovered momentarily just above the plaza, dipped its nose and then set off in a southerly direction towards the coast at great speed. As she looked up at the helicopter and its occupants, Sarah was sure that she had caught a glimpse of a familiar face peering down towards them just before it flew onwards.

'I think that may well have been Tom,' she said to Carlos,

almost not believing what she had just witnessed.

'Where?' said Carlos. 'In that helicopter? Are you sure? What the hell would he be doing in a helicopter?'

'I'm really not sure, but if it was him, I think I've just worked out where he may have headed for.'

'Where's that?' asked Carlos.

'The lighthouse, just below Teneguia. It has a helicopter landing pad and I can't think of anywhere else south of here that a helicopter could land. I think we should head for there.'

'I suppose it's worth a try,' said Carlos, slightly disappointed that Sarah was not, as yet, prepared to abandon her quest for Tom. But Carlos was also aware that their rescue mission had not been a total waste of time. For one thing, it had confirmed to him that Sarah did have feelings for him and that her decision to return to La Palma had not been totally motivated by a desire to find her husband.

'And then what?' said Carlos.

But Sarah did not reply as she strode towards their parked car. Her mind was fixed on what she was going to say to Tom when she eventually caught up with him. Relief that he was safe would no doubt be her opening conversational gambit. But what then? A full and frank explanation of why she was back on the island? Or one which told only half the story? *Perhaps*, she thought to herself, *the part about Carlos should wait until another time.*

As Carlos started the car and selected reverse so as to extricate himself from the raised area of cobbles, he noticed something strange about the fountain in the centre of the plaza. The cobbles immediately surrounding it seemed to be darker and shinier than those further away from it. But, strangest of all, issuing from the mouths of each of the three stone dolphins which formed the centrepiece of the fountain, was a grey swirling mist. Puzzled, Carlos got out of his car and beckoned Sarah to come with him. As they walked towards the fountain Carlos was sure that he could feel the ground beneath his feet gently and rhythmically resonating.

'Did you feel that?'

But, once again, Sarah did no reply. Her attention was focused on a hissing sound emanating from the fountain which momentarily reminded her of the valve on her pressure cooker back at the finca.

The vibration beneath their feet returned, but this time much stronger than before and it caused them both to pause for a moment.

'You must have felt that?' said Carlos. Sarah nodded, but yet again said nothing as her attention was still focused on the fountain.

'My God,' said Sarah as they drew closer, 'It's steam. The fountain is letting off steam!'

Instantly, the seemingly mad ramblings of the inebriated Pedro began to make sense, but before they could say or do one more thing, the ground beneath their feet began to move – upwards initially, and then from side to side, almost as if they were on a rope and plank bridge that was swaying violently in the wind. Sarah and Carlos clung to each other for a moment and then, unable to maintain their balance, began to fall towards the cobbled surface of the plaza - just as the fountain exploded into a thousand pieces, spraying boiling hot water and fist sized fragments of razor sharp granite in all directions. The blast lifted the falling Sarah and Carlos off their feet and sent them both flying several metres back from the fountain. Carlos landed, a fraction of a second before Sarah, head first, with a sickening thud on the granite cobbled surface. And, as the swirling mists of impending unconsciousness and ultimate death began to envelop him, he saw, for the last time, the figure of Sarah moving towards him and then, as his eyes closed, her image disappeared.

'Carlos!' screamed Sarah, as she crawled, on her hands and knees, towards his prostrate body.

As he lay, face down, twitching occasionally and with his right leg twisted beneath him, a small pool of blood had begun slowly forming on the cobbles of the plaza next to his concealed face.

'Carlos!' screamed Sarah again, as she attempted to place him in the recovery position and repeatedly called his name. But Carlos did not respond and as she turned him over, his wide open eyes, staring lifelessly up at the clear blue sky, instantly indicated that he was dead.

Although Sarah never lost consciousness, a combination of shock and pain caused by the scalding hot water which had sprayed the upper right hand side of her body and face, made it difficult for her to comprehend what happened to her next. Her body seemed weightless and she felt like she was rising up and being swept along as if in the current of a fast flowing river. Blurred images of buildings were racing past and she thought she could hear a muffled voice saying something to her in an unfamiliar foreign tongue, but she could not understand what it was saying. Then there were many voices. Some were shouting, others were screaming and she felt her body slowly and gently descending and then something hard and flat seemed to be beneath her. Her arm, shoulder and face felt like they were on fire, until suddenly, the pain was gone and the voices and the screaming could no longer be heard.

As the helicopter flew onwards towards Teneguia, Tom was equally perplexed and uncertain by what he had just seen below them. Was that really his wife he had seen in the plaza? What was she doing back on the island? And what was she doing here with Carlos?

But his bewilderment about his wife was soon replaced by an overpowering feeling of anxiety as the imposing sight of the volcano suddenly appeared on the horizon and Tom could feel his pulse beginning to increase as it began to loom closer and closer. Maria was also feeling increasingly tense as they approached the volcano as she knew precisely what type of eruption could result if the vent was plugged and such close proximity to this ticking time bomb was making her heart race with fear. But the professor seemed completely oblivious to the potential danger they were all in and as the helicopter reached the volcano, he was clearly more excited than afraid. As the steeply sloping flanks of Teneguia made a landing impossible, the professor ordered the pilot to circle the volcano and as they flew over its crater and then around to its southern flank, he suddenly became increasingly animated

'I knew it! I knew it! It's a lava dome!' he exclaimed, pointing to the large bulge in the crater of the volcano. 'And, my God, look at the southern flank - it's bulging too. It has to be a cryptodome! Whilst all our attention has been focused on the northern end of Cumbre Vieja, the real problem and the potentially big eruption has been inexorably building here, all the time, on the southern end of the ridge.'

But the professor's excitement was not shared by either of his two companions. En route to the volcano Maria had briefly explained to Tom what had happened at Mt St Helens when a cryptodome on the volcano's flank had slipped and fear about their close proximity to Teneguia and its newly formed bulge on its southern flank was now gripping both to the same degree.

'When do you think it will erupt?' asked Tom, somewhat nervously.

'Could be days yet,' said the professor, 'or it could happen at any minute. Eruption prediction is not, as you should have gathered by now, Señor Baxter, a precise science.'

For a brief moment, Tom felt like one of the professor's students who was being chastised for asking an inane question. He even began to mentally reprimand himself for asking such a ridiculous question and was on the verge of apologising to the professor for his stupidity, when he remembered that he was merely a former History teacher whose entire knowledge of volcanology, could, until a few days ago, have been written on the back of a postage stamp. Nevertheless, before he could stop himself, he blurted out an apology and, although seated behind the professor and therefore only able to see part of his face, was sure that he detected the sides of the professor's mouth beginning to form a smile as he did so.

'If that's the case, Professor, don't you think we should get the hell out of here as quickly as possible,' said Tom, his feelings of embarrassment being quickly subsumed by the much greater feelings of fear.

Tom was both astounded and pleased by the Professor's response.

'For once, Señor Baxter, we are of the same mind and I totally agree that we should make a hasty withdrawal to a safer location and consider our options.'

As far as Tom was concerned, the only sensible option at this point would have been to fly north as quickly as possible and not stop until they hit somewhere safe such as the British coastline, but from what he had learnt about the professor in the short period of time he had known him, the thrill seeking academic would have other, considerably less cautious, options in mind.

'We can't land on the helicopter pad near the lighthouse because, being to the south of the volcano, it will be directly in the firing line, so you'd best take us to the northern side of the volcano,' said the professor to the pilot, 'and find somewhere to land there. I suggest we head back towards Funacaliente and land in the plaza' The pilot nodded, as much in relief as in compliance, banked hard to the left, and with the helicopter now heading northwards, set a course for the short flight back to Funacaliente.

Tom's face fell at the professor's announcement, as did Maria's, who secretly also wished to put as much distance as possible between herself and the volcano, especially after the professor set about explaining to Tom what might well happen if the volcano was to erupt.

'What we are looking at,' he began, 'is potentially a Vulcanian or perhaps, more worryingly, a Vulcanian eruption with a phreatomagmatic element. In any event, it will be considerably more violent than the Strombolian type of eruption that we have been witnessing on the northern end of Cumbre Vieja during the last few days.'

Tom was on the verge of interrupting the professor and asking him for an explanation when he felt Maria's hand on his forearm as a signal not to. Having attended scores of the professor's lectures and seminars over the last three years, Maria instantly recognised when the professor was entering 'teaching mode', and knew from her own experience that any request for an explanation at this point would be futile.

'Don't panic, I'll explain when he's done,' she mouthed, in an attempt to placate an increasingly frustrated and worried looking Tom.

'The small Italian island of Vulcano,' continued the professor, 'off the coast of Sicily, provides the family name for all volcanoes and repeated eruptions on Vulcano led the Romans to believe that this island was the forge of *Vulcan*, son of Jupiter and blacksmith to the Roman gods,' said the professor

At last, some classical history, thought Tom, at the mention of names and a time period that he had some prior knowledge and understanding of. But Tom's feelings of understanding were quickly stripped away as the professor got into his geological stride.

'But the island of Vulcano also gives its name to a particular eruption style called a Vulcanian eruption. This type of eruption results from the fragmentation and explosion of a plug of lava in a volcanic conduit, or from the rupture of a lava dome formed from highly viscous andesitic or rhyolitic lava that has piled up and solidified over a vent. Vulcanian eruptions create a powerful explosion in which material can be ejected at speeds up to eight hundred miles per hour and usually begin with a series of smaller, short lived, canon like explosions.'

'A bit like someone clearing their throat before they begin a big speech,' interrupted Tom.

The professor paused for an instant as he pondered Tom's analogy which, as it appealed to his sense of the dramatic, caused him to smile, albeit briefly, before continuing.

'Their explosivity can be enhanced if the magma interacts with water in sub surface aquifers creating what is known as a phreatic eruption. The pulverisation of the lava dome and the rock surrounding the vent then produce an ash cloud which may form into a column several kilometres in height. But the real problem comes when this ash column collapses and the red hot ash and gas flows down the flanks of the volcano at speeds in excess of three hundred miles per hour in what is known as a pyroclastic flow. If the flow is large enough, and if it enters a nearby body of water such as a lake or sea, it can create a tsunami which could be as high as one hundred feet and travel at speeds in excess of five hundred miles per hour. And what I have just described is precisely the situation that we have here with regards to Teneguia. The vent is clearly plugged and, judging by the bulge on the southern flank, so too is a lateral subsidiary conduit. Magmatic pressure is inexorably increasing and from what you told us about your water supply problems a few days ago, I suspect that the magma has evaporated all the water in nearby underground aquifers and a phreatic eruption is most likely.'

'So,' interrupted Tom, 'it's a bit like a pressure cooker with a safety valve that's become stuck.'

'Almost', replied the Professor, 'But when this pressure cooker, as you call it, blows, the effects will go way beyond your kitchen, if you'll pardon me hijacking your analogy. The impact of the tsunami that it will invariably create will be felt on every surrounding island in the Canarian chain and maybe as far south as the Cape Verde Islands and the West African coast. First to succumb to the tsunami will be the islands of Tenerife and Gomera and coastal settlements such Puerto de la Brava will be totally inundated and the death toll will run into the tens of thousands. Soon after El Heirro and Gran Canaria will be hit by a slightly smaller, but nevertheless devastating tsunami, and then Lanzarote will succumb.

Then, as it travels south and east, the size of the wave will diminish to about fifty feet, but that will be more than sufficient to inundate the islands of Boa Vista and all others in the Cape Verde island chain. Once again coastal settlements will be inundated and a death toll in the thousands will result. All in all I estimate about one million people could die.'

Maria had stopped listening when the Professor had mentioned Tenerife. Her thoughts had immediately turned to that of her sister, Consuela, and as the helicopter flew onwards to Funacaliente, she knew that she urgently needed to contact her and warn her of the peril that she was in. Maria reached into her pocket to retrieve her mobile, but her face instantly contorted into a look of desperation and horror when she saw that the number of signal bars available was zero.

When the helicopter reached Funacaliente a few minutes later and hovered over the town's plaza, its occupants were startled by the scene of devastation below. Only an hour had gone by since they had last passed overhead and since then a huge fissure, perhaps a metre wide and traversing the entire length of the plaza, had opened up and steam was rising from all along its length causing the plaza to be shrouded in a grey, wet mist. All the shops and cafés were windowless, awnings were torn and tattered and some shops were missing their doors. But, strangest of all, was the gaping hole in the centre of the plaza. As the helicopter hovered directly over the spot where the fountain had once stood, Tom looked down and said,

'There used to be a fountain where that hole is and, what's really weird, is that the hole seems full of water, yet I was told that the fountain had been dry for years.'

Immediately the professor turned his attention to where Tom was looking and suddenly, and most uncharacteristically, screamed at the pilot to ascend. Somewhat startled, the pilot pulled hard on his joy stick and the helicopter rose rapidly, just high enough to avoid the huge jet of scalding hot water that suddenly erupted from the hole, narrowly missing the helicopter.

'What the hell was that?' shouted the pilot over the radio.

'It's a geyser,' shouted the professor, but Tom needed no explanation on this occasion as he had seen Old Faithful erupt in a similar fashion when visiting Yellowstone National Park some years ago.

'Stay at this altitude,' said the professor to the pilot, 'as I expect it will erupt again any second now.'

Within less than a minute, the professor's prediction was proved correct as another eruption of boiling water and steam shot at least fifty metres into the air, drenching the plaza again a few seconds later as the scalding water fell back to Earth.

'How did you know that was going to happen?' said Tom, secretly impressed by the professor's ability to so accurately predict an entirely natural event.

'Watch the water in the vent,' said the professor.

Tom looked at the small blue circle of water covering the vent. Slowly, almost imperceptibly, the water seemed to expand into a circular, blue, lens-like structure which then became increasingly more bulbous by the second. After about thirty seconds, the water had formed a large blue dome over the vent which then suddenly erupted into the air, once again showering the entire plaza with boiling hot water.

'This is worse than I expected.' said the professor, with a worried look on his face.

Maria knew instantly why the professor was concerned and, turning to Tom, said, 'How long had the fountain in Funacaliente been dry?'

'For as long as I've been living here,' replied Tom.

'Do you know when it stopped issuing water?'

'Yes, I do actually. My friend Carlos told me only the other day that the fountain ran dry just before the last eruption of Teneguia back in 1971. He said something about the magma evaporating all the water in the aquifer which supplies the fountain and turning it into steam and then the volcano erupted.'

Maria and the professor shared a knowing look which Tom noticed immediately.

'Why is that so bad?' he asked the two volcanologists.

'Because,' replied the professor, 'I believe that the recent seismic activity in this area has fractured the crust, allowing water to seep, under the influence of gravity, from a full aquifer further up the ridge, into the previously dry one under Teneguia.'

Tom remained clearly perplexed and so the professor

continued.

'Do you recall what I said previously about phreatic eruptions?' Tom nodded as the professor continued, 'In order for such an eruption to occur, there has to be a supply of underground water for the magma to super heat and turn into highly pressurised steam.'

Tom nodded again, adding, 'Just like the pressure cooker.'

'Yes, quite,' said the professor. 'Until now, that water supply has been lacking, but clearly the aquifer is now filling again, hence the geyser. I suspect we are looking at the worst scenario possible with regard to the impending eruption of Teneguia'

Maria took over the explanation at this point.

'Tom, we are now looking most definitely at a Vulcanean eruption with a phreatic element.'

'And', interjected the professor, 'the tsunami scenario I outlined is looking all the more likely too.'

At the mention of tsunamis, Maria's thoughts once again turned to that of her sister working in a beachside hotel on Tenerife. She took out her phone and for a second time checked the signal strength. 'Shit,' she hissed under her breath, when, once again, a total lack of bars was indicated.

Opting instead to text Consuela, she simply wrote;'Get to high ground now. Can't explain why, just get somewhere away from the sea straight away and stay there. Your life depends on it. Trust me.'

Then, just as the professor was turning to the pilot to ask him to radio base and relay to the authorities what was brewing, a series of cannon like blasts suddenly shook the helicopter, causing it to veer sideways.

'What the hell now?' exclaimed the pilot

'I think,' said the professor, claiming ownership of Tom's earlier analogy, 'Teneguia is clearing her throat in preparation for her big speech.'

Then, before he could say anything else, the helicopter was rocked by the shock wave of a much bigger blast. Struggling to keep control of his craft, the pilot immediately dipped the helicopter's nose and throttled the craft in order to regain some stability and then flew at top speed away from the plaza in a northerly direction.

'That's the lava dome being blown clear of the vent.' said the professor, his voice a bizarre mixture of excitement and concern. As he spoke, a huge column of grey ash and steam almost immediately began spiralling and billowing upwards and within seconds had begun to merge with the dark clouds which lay high above the volcano.

'I suspect the cryptodome will be next to go, and, if it does...' his voice trailed away and for once, the normally effusive professor went strangely quiet for a moment before continuing, 'thousands of people will die unless, of course, we can warn them of the approaching tsunami.'

'How much warning will they get?' asked Tom.

'Not very much, I'm afraid,' replied the professor.

'Travelling at a speed of five hundred miles per hour and with the rest of the Canary Islands all within one hundred to one hundred and fifty miles of the volcano, I'd say Gomera will have, at best, seven minutes before the tsunami makes landfall; Tenerife, a fraction longer at twelve minutes; El Heirro perhaps fifteen or so minutes. What's more, such is the nature of tsunamis, that in open, deep water, out to sea, the wave is barely noticeable at about a metre high and only grows to the monstrous proportions that I have described when it reaches shallower water, near the coastline. I think you get the picture, Señor Baxter.'

'So, not only will the tsunami arrive in next to no time, but you can't even see it coming until it's too late to do anything about it,' said Tom.

'That just about sums it up, Señor Baxter, although, just before the tsunami strikes, the water closest to the shore will rapidly retreat almost as if the tide has suddenly and rapidly gone out, which might give some warning to those living next to the sea, providing, of course, they are knowledgeable enough about the behaviour of tsunamis to know what's about to happen next. However, let's not forget that the cryptodome has yet to slip, so we still have a small window of opportunity to issue some kind of longer term warning, but there remains, of course, the problem of what will happen when, not if, the ash column collapses. That in itself could create a tsunami of considerable magnitude which, although not as big as a tsunami created by an outwardly exploding cryptodome, could still result in major loss of life on every island in the Canaries and beyond.' And with that the professor turned to the pilot next to whom he was sat and asked to be patched through to the Director at headquarters.

Chapter 28

As darkness began to fall and with the helicopter now landed on a small ridge just outside of Funacaliente, Tom and Maria sat looking at the glowing grey and red column of ash which had grown rapidly skywards since the lava dome had been blown off.

'You know, Maria, if it wasn't so damn deadly, you could almost describe it as beautiful.'

'I know exactly what you mean,' replied Maria, with her eyes fixed on the ash plume.

Tom coughed, and then, as he coughed again, he noticed that Maria's hair was covered with small grey specks of ash.

'Your hair!' exclaimed Tom, 'Maria, your hair is covered with ash!'

Maria reached up and ran her fingers quickly through her hair and then looked at her hands.

'Your hair is too,' said Maria, looking at Tom's head, 'and so is your jacket.'

Simultaneously, Tom and Maria's eyes were drawn, almost magnetically, back to the ash plume above the erupting volcano. Then, as they continued to watch, the plume began to change shape. Slowly at first, and then more rapidly, the plume appeared to be getting wider and wider and its height seemed to be decreasing.

'Oh my God!' cried Maria. 'It's beginning to collapse.'

And, just as the professor had earlier predicted, the red hot ash began its rapid return to Earth where it would soon form a seaward heading pyroclastic flow which, in turn, would create the deadly tsunami – that, once again, the professor had so accurately and expertly predicted.

Chapter 29

Mount Teide, Tenerife

Consuela could barely remember how she'd got there or how long
it had taken, but it was just after dusk when she arrived at the
summit of Tenerife's highest volcanic peak. She stopped her car
in the small gravel car park near to the volcano's visitor centre,
turned off the car's engine and then its headlights and sat there
in the near darkness, watching the silver light of the rising moon
shimmering on the distant Atlantic Ocean. Far below, strung out
along the rapidly darkening coastline, like a diamond encrusted
necklace, the lights of Puerto de la Brava were just beginning
to appear. Slowly, but surely, her breathing began to normalise
and her pulse rate slowed to a steady beat. Her mind was now
no longer a maelstrom of panic with her thoughts spiralling
uncontrollably round and round. Here, on the mountain top, in
her locked car, she was safe, and as a feeling of calmness began
to wrap itself around her body, she could feel the tension draining
from every pore of her being. Even the memories of how Franco
had treated her throughout their time together; memories which,
in spite of her very best efforts, she could never completely banish
from her mind, now seemed, for the moment at least, to be less
vivid and almost bearable.

Gradually her thoughts turned from the danger posed by
Franco having discovered her whereabouts, to that of the stranger
who had attacked her earlier that day. She felt no remorse or

regret for what she had done to the man and, in a strange sort of way, was actually proud of herself, because for once in her life she had not succumbed meekly to a violent attack on her person, but had fought back and even triumphed.

Perhaps, she thought, *if I had had the courage to do to Franco, what I have just done to that stranger, then I wouldn't be in the situation that I am now.*

However, whilst pleased with her new found courage, Consuela was acutely aware that what she had done to defend herself was probably a crime and knew that, before long, she would have to report her actions to the police. So she began to replay the events in her mind, slowly and carefully, ensuring that, when called upon, she would be able to relate what had happened precisely and accurately. She was also sure that the police would understand that she had been in fear of her life when the man had grabbed her, but whether or not they would understand the degree of violence that she had used to defend herself was another matter. Perhaps if she told them about Franco's mistreatment of her and why she had fled to Tenerife in the first place they would appreciate why she had reacted in the way she had. *Yes,* she thought, *the full story would have to be told if they were going to understand.*

For the first time in her life Consuela felt no fear. She felt totally in control and completely calm. It was almost as if a tremendous weight had been lifted from her shoulders and she felt free again. It had been so many years since she had felt this way; almost empowered, but above all it was so good to feel like the woman she had been before meeting Franco.

But her feeling of calmness was soon replaced by that of an irresistible tiredness. Try as she might, she could not stop her eyelids from closing. It was almost as if she had taken one of the sleeping tablets that the constant fear of Franco had forced her into taking every night for the last six months. Or, perhaps, it was just that she was still in a state of shock. But whatever it was, she just had to sleep and she knew almost instinctively that for once her dreams would not feature the brutal Franco.

As her eyes closed and the first wave of an impending deep sleep washed gently over her, she failed to notice the blue, flashing light of a police car, making its way rapidly up the winding road from the valley bottom to the mountain top.

Chapter 30

The Atlantic Ocean, Ten miles Northwest of Tenerife

Off the northwest coast of Tenerife, the crew of the fishing boat, Santa Maria de la Rosa, were busily hauling in the day's last catch of sardines. For the first time in several weeks, the fishing had been good and the crew were in buoyant mood, knowing that their wages this week would be significantly more than the pittance that they had received last week and the week before that. Jose Marco, the captain of the Santa Maria de la Rosa, was equally pleased with the day's haul and was whistling happily to himself as he turned his vessel slowly through one hundred and eighty degrees and set a south easterly course for Puerto de la Brava. Just as he completed the manoeuvre, something on the horizon to the northwest caught his eye.

Initially, Captain Marco assumed that the dark, towering, anvil shaped mass of billowing moisture, illuminated at its base by the rapidly setting sun in the far west, was simply an isolated cumulonimbus cloud. Thirty years as a fisherman in these waters had taught him that such clouds normally heralded the arrival of a storm, but as the forecast for the next twenty four hours had made no mention of bad weather approaching from the northwest, Captain Marco was puzzled by the sudden appearance of this lone cloud formation, which was possibly the tallest cumulonimbus he had ever seen. Intrigued, he slowed the engine of his vessel so that it was barely ticking over, set the automatic pilot system for a south easterly course and left the wheel house to join the rest of the crew on the aft deck. By the time he had descended the short flight of steps which led to the rear of the boat, the crew had also noticed the bizarre sight in the rapidly darkening evening sky and had stopped what they were doing and were now all staring at the strange cloud formation.

'What do you make of that, Captain?' said the first mate, with his outstretched arm pointing to the cloud which seemed to have grown even taller and wider by the time the captain had joined his crew.

'I'm not sure I know what it is,' replied Captain Marco, as his eyes focused on the base of the cloud and then slowly followed its towering form into the upper atmosphere. 'Could be an approaching cold front I suppose, but the shipping forecast made no mention of that when I tuned into it a few hours ago.'

'If that's the case,' said the first mate, 'we'll need to batten down the hatches because that's the biggest storm cloud that I've seen in all my many years at sea,' and then, shaking his head vigorously from side to side added, 'No, I don't think that's a storm cloud, Captain, it's something else, but what it is, I have no idea either.'

'Could be an eruption plume,' said a deckhand, who was standing just behind the two men. The captain and the first mate turned to face the deckhand and simultaneously said,

'Eruption? What eruption?'

'On La Palma. Cumbre Vieja has been erupting for the last few days.' replied the deckhand.

'Or it could be Teneguia,' he continued. 'We studied its last eruption when I was in school and that caused a massive column of ash that could be seen from Tenerife.'

'Maybe it is,' said the captain. 'But thankfully, that's La Palma's problem, not ours, so how about restarting the net winch and let's get these sardines back safe and sound to Puerto de la Brava.'

As the captain began walking back to the wheel house, he felt the Santa Maria de la Rosa rise a few feet in the water and tilt slightly to the port side, as if lifted by a rogue swell and then the boat sank slowly back into the otherwise calm and placid water. He paused momentarily and turned his head back towards the rear of the boat to see if the crew had also felt the boat lifting, but they were now winching in their net once again and seemed oblivious to what had just happened. Dismissing the isolated swell as just a freak of the sea, the captain lit a cigarette, inhaled deeply and returned to the wheel house where, after turning off the auto pilot system, he took control of his vessel once more. Standing at the ship's helm, with his eyes now fixed on Tenerife's barely visible coastline dead ahead, he began loudly singing a Spanish sea shanty. The song, which told of fishermen returning to their home port where their loved ones would be waiting for them on the quayside, was a particular favourite of the captains and he always sang it after a good catch as he believed it would bring him good luck on the next trip. On hearing the song, the rest of the crew soon joined in and with their collective voices ringing out over the now dark, deep waters of the Atlantic Ocean, the Santa Maria de la Rosa slowly made its way back towards Puerto de la Brava, with its crew fully expecting that their loved ones would, indeed be waiting on the quayside to welcome them home, blissfully unaware of the scene that would actually confront them when they eventually reached port.

Chapter 31

Hospital Universitario de Canarias,
Puerto de la Brava, Tenerife

It was late evening and all was quiet on the male surgical ward at the Hospital Universitario de Canarias where Jose Batista lay, now fully conscious, in a bed near to the ward's entrance, The last of the day's visitors had left about ten minutes ago and, as the two nurses on duty silently moved from bed to bed, checking the vital signs of their patients before bidding them goodnight, Jose was mentally concocting the story that he would tell the police when they came to interview him in the morning. He knew that by now they would have searched his car and found items in the boot and glove compartment that may well have suggested some kind of sinister motive for him being on the island. And, knowing police procedure, he was also certain that by now they would have ascertained his identity, checked for a criminal record and then, from his mobile phone records, discovered a link between Franco and himself. But, apart from that, he concluded, they would have nothing concrete to go on and providing that he kept to his story about trying to help a helpless female motorist, whose car had stalled at the entrance to a car park and who had misinterpreted his intentions when he had opened her car door, he was sure that he would face no charges and would soon be back on the island of La Palma.

'Business as usual,' murmured Batista to himself. He smiled, closed his eyes and with the soporific sound of waves gently washing to and fro on the beach which lay no more than a few hundred metres from his hospital bed, fell rapidly into a deep, contented sleep – a sleep from which he would never wake.

Chapter 32

The Old Town, Puerto de la Brava, Tenerife

David Silvestre stood at the entrance of his restaurant, smoking a cigarette and watching the crowds file past as they made their way to the quayside for the climax of today's festival. Apart from two elderly, retired fishermen sitting at the bar drinking brandy, the restaurant was empty. But this was of no concern to David as he knew that, as soon as the firework display which marked the end of the festival was over, his restaurant would be inundated with a wave of hungry customers.

'Thank goodness for festivals,' he murmured to himself, as he stubbed his cigarette out in an ashtray and went back inside the restaurant. The recession had hit his business hard in recent years, but this weekend of festivals should help to keep his creditors at bay, for a short while longer at least.

'The calm before the storm,' said one of the fishermen, sitting at the bar and gesturing towards the harbour.

'Yes, I hope so,' replied David, as he went from table to table ensuring each had been set correctly.

'The town is packed this evening, so you should make a tidy profit,' said the other old fisherman.

'Profit, what's that when it's at home?' laughed David, as he went behind the bar to pour himself a drink. 'I'll be happy if I can cover this week's bills from tonight's and tomorrow's takings and anything else will be a bonus.'

David offered the men another drink and added, much to the approval of both men, 'Don't worry, it's on the house.'

'Are you not going to watch the burning of the sardine?' asked David.

'Not likely,' said one of the fishermen. 'I'd much rather stay here and drink your brandy than be pushed and shoved about by a whole load of drunken tourists. Besides, it's not like the old days when the festival actually meant something. What's the point of blessing a fish when there's hardly any fishing boats left, let alone sardines in the sea. No, today it's all about tourism and I don't want any part of it.' David nodded in agreement, but secretly was glad that this particular tourist attraction was helping to steer his business through troubled economic waters.

As the three men continued their conversation about festivals, amicably exchanging points of view for and against them, directly below the bar, in the restaurant's kitchen, Head Chef, Isabella Marco, was marshalling her staff with her usual authority and efficiency. She was acutely aware of the financial situation that her employer's restaurant was in and was determined to ensure that everything ran as smoothly and, as profitably, as possible during this evening's service – not just for his sake, but for her own as well, as she, too, was facing financial difficulties following weeks of poor catches by her husband's fishing boat.

'Is the paella ready?' shouted Isabella, struggling to make herself heard over the noise of clattering pans and general commotion that exists in any busy kitchen just prior to the commencement of service.

'Si, Concinera,' replied a young sous chef, wiping beads of perspiration from his forehead with the back of his hand.

'And are all the starters done?' Isabella barked, without looking up from the small saucepan that she was frantically sliding backwards and forwards over a flaming hob.

'Si, Concinera,' replied a commie chef from the far end of the kitchen.

'Buena torreon ir,' she replied, urging her staff to keep up the good work.

With all going smoothly in the kitchen and with her staff focused on the final preparations for the evening's service, Isabella took the opportunity to step outside into the small cobbled courtyard which lay to the rear of the kitchen. Compared to the heat and steam of the kitchen, the night air seemed relatively cool and Isabella drank in several refreshing lungfuls before taking her mobile phone from the food stained pocket in the front of her otherwise immaculate chef's whites. Isabella checked her messages and was pleased to see that her husband, Marco, had sent her a voicemail.

'Shit,' cursed Isabella, when, because of her position below street level, she saw that she had no signal on her phone and was unable to listen to his message. But, knowing that she would be able to secure a stronger signal if she went up to the restaurant's rooftop terrace and, confident that her kitchen staff could cope without her for a minute or two, Isabella made her way towards the bottom of the metal fire escape that led up to the roof. A minute later, perched high above the cobbled streets of Puerto de la Brava, Isabella sat down at a table and began listening to her husband's message. She smiled as she heard him excitedly tell her about the day's bumper catch of sardines and how he would treat her when he returned to port later that evening. As she listened to the remainder of the message, she could also hear the sound of the crowd cheering on the quayside and it reminded Isabella that she still had work to do that evening. But as she turned to return to the kitchen, something, far out to sea, caught her eye. At first she thought it was simply the light of the full moon, illuminating the distant horizon and creating an almost fluorescent, white, ragged line, far out to sea. But as she stood and watched it more closely, the white line seemed to be getting rapidly larger and larger and closer and closer to the shore. Puzzled by this, Isabella decided to watch it for a moment longer before going back down the staircase; a decision, which, unbeknown to Isabella at that point in time, was one that would ultimately save her life,

A short distance from the restaurant, the quayside was a cacophony of noise and a kaleidoscope of colour. Almost the entire population of the town, together with hundreds of tourists, had congregated there to witness the climactic phase of the day's festivities. As the music from folk bands and the smoke from sardines being grilled over charcoal filled the night air, all around the packed quayside the excited crowd were waiting for the arrival of the evening's main attraction.

And, amidst the throng, there was no group more excited than the Simmons family from England. This was the final evening of their holiday and they were looking forward to seeing something really memorable to end their stay on the island and, as suggested by the owner of their hotel, what could be more memorable than watching a highly decorated twelve foot long papier mache sardine being carried aloft through the packed streets, followed by wailing men dressed in drag and then watching the sardine being blessed with lighter fuel-cum-holy water, set alight and then lowered into the sea.

The fact that their hotelier was the brother-in-law of the town's tourism officer who had organised the festival, was something that he, of course, omitted to tell the Simmons family, but he did take the time to explain the historical significance of the festival as he sold them three discounted tickets. And, also on the advice of the hotelier, the family had arrived at the quayside early so as to ensure they got a good view of the sardine burning ceremony, and by early evening they were perfectly placed, on a bench, right on the edge of the quay and in good time to witness what was destined to be the most memorable festival in the history of the town.

Their seven year old daughter, Amy, was particularly looking forward to the festival as this was her first trip abroad. And as she sat on the bench, literally trembling with excitement, she was already mentally composing what she would write at the start of the new school year, when she would be asked to produce the inevitable, '*What did you do on your holiday*', essay.

Since her father had been made redundant a couple of years ago, family holidays for the Simmons had largely been confined to a week's stay in a caravan on the Essex coast and for the last two Septembers she had dreaded having to read out her essay to her class mates. But, owing to her father's small win on the lottery, *This year would be different,* thought Amy to herself, because this year, she would be describing the colours, the noise, the smells and above all, the burning of a twelve foot long sardine in a story which she was pretty sure none of her class mates would be able to match.

As the Simmons family sat waiting for the festival's climax, a man with a megaphone on a podium to their right began whipping the crowd into a frenzy as the arrival of the sardine drew closer. Suddenly, a cheer went up from the people furthest back from the quayside as they caught the first glimpse of the sardine and its entourage of burly, bearded fishermen, dressed in brightly coloured flamenco dresses and sporting headgear so outlandish in design that it would not have been out of place at a Brazilian carnival. Their exaggerated wailing was soon drowned out by the growing cheers and raucous laughter of the crowds packed onto the quayside and, as the Simmons family joined in with the celebrations, Amy looked up at her father and said,

'Thanks, Dad, for the best holiday ever.'

Slowly, but surely, the sardine and its entourage made its way through the heaving mass of humanity and eventually reached the edge of the quay where, dressed as a priest, was the town's officer for tourism. After mumbling a few words in what was supposed to be Latin, he made the sign of the cross, sprinkled the sardine with lighter fluid, cunningly disguised to look like a vessel of Holy Water, and gave the signal for the sardine to be lowered into the water. The man with the megaphone was giving a running commentary for the benefit of those who were at the back of the quayside and who were unable to see precisely what was happening, but no such commentary was needed by the Simmons family who were ideally placed to see every facet of the ceremony.

'We were right to get here when we did,' said Mr Simmons to his wife, who replied with a rapid nodding of her head.

Mr Simmons put his arms simultaneously around the waist of his wife and shoulders of Amy and allowed himself a small, self-satisfied smile as he thought to himself: *This year was going to be a new beginning for his family. Their financial problems were now over thanks to their lottery win and, what's more, he had an interview for a new job scheduled for when they returned to England.*

Amy was smiling too as she mentally composed another paragraph of her soon to be written essay and felt certain that the finished piece of work would make her the most envied girl in the class come September.

As the sardine bobbed up and down on the calm, sheltered water of the harbour, a sudden silence descended on the crowded quayside as those who had witnessed the ceremony before knew that it was about to reach its climax. With much dramatic effect, the 'priest' took a match from his cassock pocket, picked a paper torch from the table upon which he had placed the vessel of 'holy water', lit the torch and then, with a few more words of supposed Latin and another sign of the cross, dropped the now blazing torch onto the sardine in the water below. This was the signal for the crowd to cheer loudly once more and the man with the megaphone began singing an old fisherman's song, the words of which were known only to the locals, but that did not prevent many of the more drunken tourists from attempting to sing along with them.

At the restaurant David heard the renewed cheering of the crowd and knew that within the hour his troubled restaurant would be packed to the rafters and his staff would be rushed off their feet. The cheering of the crowd was also the signal for the two elderly fishermen at the bar to finish their drinks and begin to make their way home, mumbling about tourists and the old days as they stumbled out of the restaurant's door and onto the currently empty street.

'Buenos Noches,' said one to David, without turning, but with his arm raised in a gesture of farewell.

'I hope you make a fortune tonight, David', said the other.

'Let's hope so. Same time tomorrow, gentlemen?'

'Si and let's hope the drinks will be free all night.'

'We'll see, we'll see,' said David, as he waved goodbye to both men.

At the quayside, the sardine was now fully ablaze, bobbing gently up and down and seemingly dancing a duet with the reflections of the flames on the placid water of the harbour. As it burned, a plume of white smoke spiralled slowly upwards into the dark night and then, borne by a gentle onshore breeze, began to mingle with the haze of barbeque smoke which hung over the quayside like an autumn mist.

The cheering crowd watched the burning sardine intently,

waiting for the last flame to fade and die as this would signal the start of the firework display. But, for some inexplicable reason, the burning effigy was not behaving as normal. Rather than remain close to the harbour wall, where it had been gently placed a few minutes earlier, the blazing sardine seemed to be drifting slowly, and then more rapidly, towards the centre of the harbour. Then it appeared to pick up even more speed and began moving towards the harbour entrance, with the smoke and flames now trailing increasingly horizontally in its wake.

One by one, the crowd closest to the edge of the quay stopped cheering and stood, with their mouths agog, in total silence. Those that couldn't see exactly what was happening also soon fell silent as they sensed and heard the change in the behaviour of those at the water's edge.

For their part, the Simmons family were oblivious to the unusual behaviour of the burning sardine and assumed that the sudden quietness of the crowd was all part of the ceremony.

'I wonder what's going to happen next?' said Amy to her parents.

'Haven't the foggiest,' replied Mr Simmons. 'But I reckon it's going to be pretty spectacular judging by how quiet the crowd has gone.'

It was at this point that the man with the megaphone sought to reassure the now increasingly quiet crowd with a comment about someone having attached an outboard motor to the sardine and, although many people laughed, albeit nervously, the sardine continued moving away from the quayside and soon it had passed through the outer harbour gates and to the open sea beyond. After a few more minutes, it was just a small speck of light many hundreds of metres from the crowded, but now totally silent, quay.

In the darkness it was difficult to see what was happening to the actual water in the harbour, but some near the front of the crowd began to notice that the level was dropping, almost imperceptibly to begin with, then more noticeably, as items that had long lain submerged on the bottom of the harbour began to emerge from the murky depths. Old car tyres, rusty chains, the rotten hull of a scuppered fishing boat and other discarded items of marine paraphernalia gradually began to appear. As the water level continued to drop, fishing boats moored on the far side of the harbour began to lean at increasingly acute angles and unsecured items on their decks rolled from them, landing silently on the now exposed mud of the harbour bottom where fish, stranded by the rapidly retreating water, flapped pathetically.

'Look!' shouted someone, pointing at the drained harbour. 'All the water has gone.'

As he spoke, an isolated gust of wind suddenly started blowing items of litter around the quayside. Then, as the wind grew in strength, ropes which supported the colourful pennants and fairy lights arranged around the edge of the quay began to sway backwards and forwards, gently at first, and then with an ever increasing tempo. Soon the wind had become so strong that people were forced to clutch their hats to their heads and, on the now eerily quiet quayside, it could even be heard whistling through the rigging of the fishing boats which now lay, like beached whales, on their sides, in the wet, glinting mud of the harbour bottom.

Puzzled and then increasingly worried looks had now replaced the previously happy and carefree ones on the faces of the crowd. Even the Simmons family sensed that something unusual was happening and soon became concerned as well.

'Something's not right,' said Mr Simmons, turning towards his wife and daughter. 'I've never seen a harbour empty of water so quickly.' 'And nor,' he said, looking at the people all around him, 'have any of these locals. I think we should get out of here as quickly as possible.'

But the mass of people behind them made any hasty retreat difficult and, try as they might, they could not seem to make any progress in their attempt to distance themselves from the water's edge.

'Keep going,' said Mr Simmons, as he held the hand of his daughter and literally pulled her through the mass of people.

'Dad, you're hurting my wrist!' said Amy. 'Please let go.'

But Mr Simmons was oblivious to her plea and, tightening his grip on his daughter's wrist still further, he continued to drag her behind him, using his other hand to push those in front of him out of the way. Such was his determination to get away from the water's edge that he didn't hear his wife calling to him to slow down as she became increasingly separated from the pair, nor did he hear the new sound which joined that of the now howling wind.

It was a sound that everybody standing on the quay had heard countless times before. A sound that usually conjures up happy memories of lazy days spent sunbathing on a beach or walking along the shoreline with one's family. A sound that is so commonplace and innocuous that few had ever given it a second thought. It was the sound that the sea makes as it approaches the shore and slowly builds into a wave and then crashes harmlessly onto the beach.

But there were some on the quay, especially the elderly fishermen, whose senses were more in tune with the sound and behaviour of the wind and sea and who knew that this was not the sound of a gentle summer wave or one that swashes harmlessly up a beach and then runs slowly back to the sea. They knew that the roaring sound, which had begun to drown out the howling wind, was the unmistakable sound that a rogue wave makes when it approaches a shoreline.

And, as the silent crowd stood open mouthed and bewildered,

with their eyes focused on the waterless harbour below, the old fishermen knew that, just offshore, the sea was rapidly sucking water, rocks and pebbles from the near shore in order to fuel its unstoppable growth into an onrushing and towering, glassy green wall of water whose ragged, tooth like crest of froth and foam, was fast approaching and about to devour the outer harbour wall. They knew, too, that there was nothing that could be done to stop what was about to happen. So they waited, not in ignorance like the rest of the crowd, but in silence, resigned to their fate.

As the wave approached the harbour, it rapidly grew in height, dwarfing the outer harbour wall. For a split second, it seemed to hang high in the air above the wall, as if it had stopped and was considering what to do next, and then it toppled forward, crashing downwards with a huge boom, instantaneously swamping the outer harbour and drawing the attention of the crowds packing the quayside. In a matter of seconds, previously marooned fishing boats rose up from the harbour mud and began moving swiftly towards the inner harbour, spiralling madly around and around in the maelstrom of white foaming water. Next, the wave surged through and over the entrance to the inner harbour and began rushing at great speed towards the quayside.

The first scream pierced the night air. It was quickly followed by another, and then another, and within seconds the scene on the quayside was one of complete and utter pandemonium. Desperate to escape, people were pushing and climbing over one another to get away from the water's edge. Some fell and were trampled underfoot by the stampeding crowd; others just stood motionless, transfixed by the sight of what was approaching and too terrified to move.

But any attempt to escape proved futile as, within less than ten seconds, the wave had reached the quayside and what was once a place of noise, light and laughter was soon transformed into a swirling and heaving mass of water, bodies, debris and darkness. The handful of people who somehow managed to grab onto something to stop themselves from being swept away, soon found that their strength was no match for that of the sea and, as their grip weakened, they too were picked up and washed towards the buildings lining the harbour. Scores of people were swept like wet rag dolls through the windows of harbour side restaurants and bars, the shattered glass shredding their bodies as they were carried inside and pinned against interior walls by the sheer force of the water; others were hurled into the walls of buildings and pulverised by the unrelenting mass of inflowing water or carried like flotsam at great speed through the narrow streets and into the lower part of the town. In the total darkness that had now descended on the quayside, the cries of drowning people and those of children separated from their parents rang out and were carried by the wind towards the town, where shop owners and restauranteurs, unaware of what was happening but a few hundred metres away from them, waited, in expectation of a busy and profitable evening's custom.

####

As David stood at the entrance to his restaurant, waiting to see the first rocket from the firework display arc overhead and then explode into a million golden flecks of light silhouetted against the dark night sky, he was puzzled as to why the display had yet to begin. Even more puzzling was the lack of people in the street outside his restaurant. Usually, within no more than five minutes of the burning ceremony finishing, he would have expected to hear the excited voices of groups of people who, in order to secure a seat in a restaurant, had forgone the fireworks display and were making their way back up the steep hill into the town centre. But all seemed strangely quiet; too quiet, in fact. He could, however, hear some noise from the quay, but it sounded different to the noise that he had heard earlier in the evening. It was the sort of noise that you might hear on a stormy night when the wind whistles through the rigging of moored fishing boats and waves crash against the harbour wall and certainly not the sort of sound you would associate with a balmy night in summer. But his puzzlement turned to concern when he heard what sounded very much like a scream drifting on the night air up from the quayside and then another and another. He stepped out into the cobbled street in order to see what was happening further down the street and stopped and stared in horror. Rapidly coming towards him was a small boat, carried on the crest of a wall of water which was as high as the first floor windows of the buildings either side of the street. As it advanced, the wall of water was scattering and then swallowing up all that lay before it. Restaurant tables, chairs, signage displaying menus and even parked motor cycles were swept up and then devoured by this roaring mass of froth, foam and dark green water. Initially, he couldn't comprehend what he was witnessing. A boat, on a wave, coming up a steep hill, engulfing everything in its path and leaving total destruction in its wake. It just didn't compute; it was too bizarre. But by the time that he realised what was coming towards him with the speed of an express train, it was too late – for him, and the two old fishermen, who had loitered outside the restaurant after leaving earlier, smoking and recollecting the old days. All three were swallowed up by the rapidly advancing watery wall of death. Then it smashed its way through the windows of his restaurant, surged through the dining room and down into the cellar where the kitchens were located. What had once been a place of warmth and laughter as the chefs busily prepared meals for the soon to be full restaurant, was quickly transformed into a dark and silent underwater tomb with kitchen utensils, food and bodies floating aimlessly about like exhibits in a dimly lit aquarium.

As the wave surged onwards into the narrow cobbled streets of the old town, it became constricted and grew in height and windows and balcony doors of second floor apartments now proved to be no match against the roaring mass of water as it burst through them, flushing furniture from rooms and people from their beds.

Soon the on rushing water reached the middle of the town and the more open plaza. Here the water level subsided slightly but then grew in height again as more and more water piled into the square. Armed now with everything that it had picked up from the lower town, the swirling water smashed into buildings, using cars, motor cycles and even bodies as battering rams against their walls and windows. The statues in the centre of the plaza were soon toppled and swept away as the wave continued its unstoppable charge through the streets of the town destroying everything in its path and it was only when it reached the upper town, that the steepness of the roads and the influence of gravity began to slow its advance.

Then, slowly, almost imperceptibly, just as if a plug had been pulled from a bath, the water level began to fall and retreat back to the sea, taking with it much, but not all, of the debris that it had gathered en route. Cars, motorbikes and even boats were the first items to be deposited by the retreating mass of putrid smelling water. Their mangled and broken remains were left dripping and perched at crazy angles in the most unlikely of places. Their owners were nowhere to be seen and whether or not they had been sucked from their vehicles by the raging torrent and then drowned or mercifully been away from them when the wave struck, was impossible to tell.

As the water slowly retreated back towards the sea, it left the once vibrant and brightly lit town of Puerto de la Brava in almost total darkness with only the sound of dripping water and the pitiful cries for help from a few badly injured survivors punctuating the otherwise total silence that now hung, like a shroud, over the town.

####

By dawn of the next day, the water had all but gone and the full extent of the destruction and death that the tsunami had caused was clearly evident. Tables, chairs, beds, children's toys, baby's prams and all manner of personal belongings formed a slowly heaving, deep, multi-coloured floating crust on the surface of the water in the harbour and rigid bodies, some already beginning to bloat, bobbed up and down amongst the debris. Within the town corpses hung like wet, tattered rags from the railings which, presumably, they had desperately clung to in an attempt to save themselves; their broken arms and legs twisted and entwined within the bars and wrought iron work. There was not a shop, or restaurant, or home that still possessed a ground floor door and water poured in mini waterfalls from first and second floor balconies and windows. Fishing nets hung limply from road signs many hundreds of metres from the harbour and dead fish lay rotting, in their thousands, on every road and pavement.

The smell of sewage, mixed with sea water, filled the early morning air, as did the cries for help from people stranded in attics or on roof tops. And as the sun rose higher over the hills immediately behind Puerto de la Brava and began to warm the sodden remains of the town, the odour of death joined that of sewage and sea water.

And floating amongst all the flotsam and jetsam was a small notebook. Its pages had been welded together into a sodden block of papier mache and whatever had been written on them was now lost forever, but the name written neatly in bright pink ink on the front of the notebook could still be read however. It said; Amy Simmons, My Holiday Notebook.

By late morning the sky above the town had gradually filled with rescue helicopters, hovering overhead and winching to safety those who had somehow managed to scramble on to roof tops including, still dressed in her now sodden Chef's whites, the bedraggled figure of Isabella Marcos, whose decision to listen to her husband's voicemail from the roof patio of the restaurant had almost certainly saved her life.

Just outside of Puerto de la Brava's harbour, a hospital ship from the Spanish navy was now moored and a constant stream of small craft scuttled to and fro between the harbour and the ship. And amongst the flotilla of rescue boats was the Santa Maria de la Rosa. Its ashen faced crew had long since stopped singing about joyful reunions with loved ones and dreaming of bulging pay packets. Now, in total silence, they cast their nets and hauled aboard the corpses that floated, in their hundreds, all around them. And as each body was landed and laid gently on the deck of the Santa Maria de la Rosa, the fishermen looked anxiously at every grey, lifeless face, hoping desperately that it did not belong to a family member or friend, before then making the sign of the cross and covering each body with a piece of old, green, oil stained tarpaulin. Captain Marcos was especially anxious as each bloated and stiff corpse was hauled aboard his fishing boat. His wife's mobile phone number was registering as unobtainable and, given where she worked, close to the quayside, and as she had not replied to his earlier message, he could only assume, that she, like hundreds of others, had perished when the tsunami had struck Puerto de la Brava.

Whilst bodies were being recovered from outside of the

harbour, a regiment from the Spanish Marine Corps had been charged with the equally gruesome task of recovering the dead from within it. As they slowly picked their way in their inflatable dinghies through the debris choked water, picking up corpses as they went, it was soon apparent that the task was going to require a much bigger number of troops than had been assigned, so by the end of the day an additional regiment had been drafted in to assist them. But as day turned to night, and as news flooded in of how other towns and cities had been affected by the tsunami, not just along the northern coast of Tenerife, but along the coastline of every other island in the Canaries and along much of the west coast of Africa, it soon became apparent to the Spanish government, and the rest of the developed world, that this was rapidly shaping up to be a disaster of truly gargantuan proportions. Offers of assistance came from all over the western world and, within less than forty eight hours, aircraft carriers and hospital ships from nearly every navy in the European Union had converged on the Canary Islands, along with others from the United States, Japan and Australia.

Predictably enough, reporters from every news station and paper in the northern hemisphere soon arrived on the scene. Some, who had been covering the eruption of Cumbre Vieja on La Palma, had only a short distance to travel and were the first to arrive, but this time they had something considerably more substantial to relay to their audiences back home and, as expected, phrases such as Armageddon and the Apocalypse peppered every news report.

In the following days the death toll steadily mounted and soon there was talk of this disaster being on a par with the Indonesian Boxing Day tsunami of 2004. But, thankfully, the rapid mobilisation and intervention of rescue forces from so many countries managed to keep the final death toll in the tens, rather than hundreds, of thousands. Even so, the impact that the tsunami had on all aspects of life in the Canary Islands, both in the short and the long term, was immense and it would be many years before the island group began to return to any semblance of normality.

Chapter 33

Mount Teide, Tenerife

Consuela woke with a start. Her car was bathed in a blue, pulsating light and the crackling sound of the police car's radio punctuated the silence of the deserted car park.

A policeman got out of the car and, with one hand on the pistol that was strapped to his belt, and the other holding a powerful torch, began walking slowly towards her car. Consuela could hear the gravel beneath the policeman's feet crunching as he drew closer, shining the torch beam on the windscreen of her car as he approached. Blinded by the brightness of the light, Consuela shielded her eyes with the back of her hand and instantly felt her pulse began to quicken. The policeman tapped the driver's window with the torch and asked her to unlock the car door and get out of the vehicle. Consuela's pulse was now racing and her chest felt tight, making it difficult to catch her breath. For a fleeting second a feeling of déjà vu gripped her, but it quickly disappeared and she dutifully obeyed the policeman's instruction and opened her car door and stepped out into the spotlight of the policeman's torch. With the beam now shining directly in her eyes, she was unable to see the policeman's face, but felt her legs buckle and almost virtually collapsed to the ground when she heard a familiar voice say,

'I thought I'd find you here'.

It was Gomez.

'I was worried about you and, when I hadn't heard from you, I rang the hotel and Adrienne told me that you'd had a visitor and were in trouble.'

'Did, did she tell you what the trouble was?' stammered Consuela.

'No. Just that you were in trouble and needed my help.'

'I've done something terrible.'

'I know,' said Gomez. 'We were called to the car park by the attendant just after the assault and have been looking for the attacker ever since.'

'How did you know it was me?' asked Consuela.

'You left a hotel pen at the scene and the car park attendant gave us a vehicle registration number which, when I ran it through the computer, turned out to be yours.'

Consuela hung her head, half in admission and half in contrition.

'This is one hell of a mess,' said Gomez, and then continued, 'and I think you need to tell me what this is all about; from the very beginning and don't leave anything out.'

His voice had an edge to it that she had never heard before. It wasn't quite official, but equally, it wasn't how he normally spoke to her and it was clear that she needed to tell him the whole sorry tale, irrespective of how painful and difficult that might be.

So, as they took a seat on a nearby bench, Consuela began to tell Gomez the story of her time with Franco and the treatment that she had endured throughout her marriage to him and, as she spoke, at one point she lifted the back of her blouse so that he could see the marks left from cigarettes being stubbed out on her torso. This was the first time that she had ever shown her scars to anyone and, although Gomez winced when he saw them, he didn't say anything, but simply nodded for her to continue. Then she told him what had happened at the traffic lights and in the multi storey car park. Gomez sat listening, in perfect silence, but from time to time she could see him clenching and unclenching his fists, especially when she told him about her mistreatment at the hands of Franco. Several times she had to pause, because the memories of her time with Franco and the horror of the attack by Batista were almost too painful to relate.

Dawn was breaking when she eventually finished telling her story. Afterwards they both sat in complete silence for a long time, staring out at the sea and watching the sun rise in the east, slowly illuminating the dark, brooding clouds on the distant horizon. Then, as individual shafts of light merged and grew in luminosity, the darkness of night was soon replaced with the pale yellow light of early morning and the first glints of sunlight began to illuminate the calm waters of the distant ocean.

Gomez was first to break the silence. He put his arm around her shoulders and said, 'I have some news that will hopefully make you feel a bit safer; Franco is missing and presumed dead.'

'But how?'

'The villa where he was living, in the Los Llanios Valley, was consumed by a lava flow and we believe that he was in it when it happened.'

'Lava flow, what lava flow?'

'Didn't you know? Cumbre Vieja has erupted and destroyed large areas on the western side of the island and especially the Los Llanios Valley.'

Consuela had heard about the earthquakes on La Palma, but in her panic and fear about Franco's presumed presence on the island, seemed to have completely missed all else that had been happening.

'Did you find his body?'

'No, and it's unlikely that we ever will, but rest assured we have it on good authority that he was in the villa and he won't be terrorising you ever again.'

'And what about the man who attacked me. Who was he?'

'We believe that he was a private detective in the employ of Franco and presumably was here to ....'

Gomez' voice trailed away, not wishing to tell Consuela what might have been his motive for coming to the island.

'To kill me,' said Consuela, finishing his sentence for him.

'That's a distinct possibility, but we'll never know for certain and he will not be telling us anything, that's for sure.'

'Why? Is he dead as well?' asked Consuela, with fear etched across her face as the memory of what she had done came flooding back.

'Fortunately, he's still alive, but we don't expect him to tell us the truth about what he had precisely been paid to do, or even that he was actually in the employ of Franco as we only have circumstantial evidence linking the two men. But this morning we will be going to the hospital to interview him and, now that you've told me the background, could charge him with your attempted kidnap. We won't be able to make it stick, but it'll make him think twice about pressing charges against you.'

'So where does that leave me?'

'Well, we're going to need a statement from you and then it'll be up to the prosecutor to decide what happens next. But after you've told me about Franco, I think the worst you can expect will be a charge of aggravated assault – if, Batista decides to press charges, that is, which is unlikely. By the way, Adrienne said something about a letter that you had pushed under your door. Do you still have it, as it could prove useful in establishing a link between Franco and Batista?'

Consuela nodded. 'Yes, it's in the glove compartment of my car. I was actually bringing it to the station when he tried to .... '

Now it was Consuela's turn for her voice to trail away, as the memory of the attack returned. She shuddered slightly and Gomez held her a little closer.

'Don't worry, everything's going to be fine. Trust me.'

Gomez smiled slightly to himself as he realised that this was the first time in his career that he had ever placed his arm around a suspect's shoulders and told them not to worry as he interviewed them. *First time for everything,* he thought to himself as he stood up and, pointing to his police car, indicated to Consuela that it was time to return to Puerto de la Brava.

Consuela nodded, and as they both walked towards the car, she felt the phone in her pocket pulse three times and then pulse three times more. Instantly she knew that her sister Maria had sent her a text message, but, realising that this was not the best time to read yet another excuse from her sister about how she was too busy at work to come to visit her in Tenerife, she reached into her jacket pocket, felt for the power button, and turned her phone off.

'Consuela,' said Gomez, 'as this is official business, at this stage at least, you're going to have to leave your car here and come in mine to the police station.'

'That's fine, I understand completely.'

'If you give me the keys to your car, when we get to the station I'll get someone to drive it back to the hotel car park.'

At the mention of the hotel, Consuela felt herself shudder slightly as memories of the letter and the phone call came flooding back for a split second.

As they drove down the steep winding road which runs from the summit of the mountain back into Puerto de la Brava, neither Consuela nor Gomez spoke a word. Both were too deep in thought. As Consuela stared out of the police car's window her thoughts were mainly focused on all that had recently happened to her, whereas Gomez was more concerned about what now lay ahead for Consuela and he was still unsure as to whether or not he should reveal the extent of his relationship with her. As the car rounded the final hairpin of the road, emerging from the mist which shrouded the upper slopes of the mountain and into the now brilliant early morning sunshine, the coastline came into view, but what confronted him suddenly caused Gomez to break the silence and contemplative calm of their journey.

'My God, Consuela! What's happened to the coast and, more to the point, where's the town gone?'

But before Consuela could look to see what had so alarmed Gomez, he brought the car to a rapid stop and, without saying anything else, quickly got out and ran to the roadside where he stood looking down at the coastline below. Consuela followed him in total bewilderment until she, too, could see what had caused him to stop so suddenly.

Both stood in total silence for a minute as they struggled to comprehend the scene that confronted them. The coastline seemed to have completely changed in shape and familiar land marks like the harbour seemed to have disappeared from the face of the Earth.

'What the hell has gone on?' said Gomez, without turning his gaze from the scene below. 'I can't see where the harbour should be.'

'And the road along the seafront seems to have disappeared too and look at the sea, it's not blue like it should be but it's …..'

Consuela struggled to find the words that could somehow describe the heaving mass of multi coloured debris that lay on the surface of the sea, lapping gently against the shoreline, from one end of the town to the other.

'I can see the church spire where the sea front should be,' said Gomez, 'but I can't see the church itself and where have all the shops and restaurants that should be next to it gone?'

Consuela didn't reply, but just shook her head in disbelief.

'I'm going to radio the station and see what the hell's been going on,' said Gomez, as he turned and started walking quickly back to his car.

Consuela heard him, but remained by the roadside and tried to see where her hotel should be in the chaotic scene below, but without any visual points of reference such as the promenade or the beach, she just could not see it.

Behind her she could hear Gomez desperately trying to make contact with the police station, but the only sound that came back to him was the crackle of interference and a high pitched whine.

'It's useless,' he said, as Consuela returned to join him at the car. 'The radio's dead or nobody's there to pick up.'

There was a moment's silence as they both simultaneously recalled the absence of familiar land marks when they had looked down from the mountain a minute ago. Neither had seen the normally imposing Town Hall where the police headquarters were located, and it slowly began to dawn on them that whatever had obliterated the harbour side area, had also destroyed the police station.

'I couldn't see the town's hospital either,' said Consuela, breaking the silence which now hung heavily over her and Gomez. 'What has happened to all the sick and elderly people?'

'God knows what has happened down there, but if it's what I think it is, then the likelihood is that they're all dead, along with, of course, our friend, Batista, who was being treated there for the injuries that you inflicted on him,' said Gomez, and then continued, 'which, hard though it may sound, does rather nicely resolve the situation that you were in.'

'What do you think has happened?' asked Consuela, almost dreading what Gomez would say in reply.

But Gomez didn't reply immediately. He just stared intently

into the distance, shaking his head slowly from side to side and then said, 'We need to get back to town and see if we can be of any assistance to those that have survived it'

'Survived what?' persisted Consuela.

'I'm not sure,' said Gomez, reaching for his ignition key, 'but we're going to find out very soon, that's for sure.'

As Gomez started the car, Consuela reached into her pocket to turn on her phone and within a few seconds it began to pulse repeatedly. This time she had no reservations about reading her messages and as she scrolled through them she came across the message from Maria. At first she was perplexed by its content, but as they drew closer to the outskirts of Puerto de la Brava and began to see the scale of the devastation that the tsunami had wrought, it rapidly dawned on her what she had been trying to warn her about. She read the message out loud to Gomez and he, too, instantly made the connection, saying,

'Yes, it's what I half suspected. I think she was trying to warn you about an approaching tsunami,' and then, nodding his head in the direction of the chaos that was now visible in front of them, said, 'and it looks like she was right too.'

'But I never got the warning as I was too busy trying to escape Batista. That's why I drove up here; to get as far away from him as possible.'

Gomez was silent for a moment before turning to Consuela and saying, 'I think, in a bizarre sort of way, your ex-husband and whatever he had asked Batista to do to you, has inadvertently helped to save your life.'

And as the first of the rescue helicopters could be heard overhead, Consuela nodded and replied, 'Yes, I think you're right. And, what's more, in an equally weird sort of way, they've also helped to save your life too.'

Chapter 34

Hospital de San Lazaro, Seville, Spain

Where the hell am I? thought Sarah, as she opened her eyes and rapidly scanned her surroundings. She was in bed, for sure, but which bed and why was she in such agony? Sarah tried to sit up. But as she did so, her face and upper body were immediately racked with such excruciating pain that she was forced to slump back down, and lay there, panting for breath, for several minutes before eventually realising that she was in hospital. And in an instant, the memory of the events that had put her there began to crystallise in her mind.

'Carlos! Oh my God Carlos!' she called out, drawing the attention of a nurse who was sitting at a desk at the far end of the ward.

'Are you alright señora?' asked the nurse, as she rose from her seat and began walking quickly towards Sarah's bed.

But Sarah was unaware of the nurse's question or even her presence when she arrived, a few seconds later, at Sarah's bedside and began checking the monitors which surrounded it.

'Oh my God.' Sarah repeated. 'Where's Carlos?'

Ignorant about who Sarah was referring to, the nurse continued to check the monitors, issuing reassuring words in Spanish as she did so.

The sound of the nurse's voice did little to calm the feeling of blind panic that was coursing through Sarah's veins, but it did help her to realise that she was still somewhere in Spain and that the events of the last few days had not been a nightmare, but were, in fact, real.

'You've been badly burnt,' said the nurse, as she adjusted the saline drip which was attached to Sarah's uninjured left arm.

Sarah tried to lift her right arm so that she could feel her face, but the excruciating pain returned and she was forced to rapidly drop her arm back on to the starched, white covers of her bed.

'Please señora, try not move, as you will not help the healing process and could damage the skin grafts.'

'Skin grafts? What skin grafts?' said Sarah, as a new wave of pain and panic washed over her.

'The doctors have had to repair the damage to your arm and ….' the nurse's voice trailed away as she tried to avoid saying the word, but after a brief pause, continued, 'face, using skin from your thighs and buttocks.'

'My face,' cried Sarah, once again reaching for the side of her face, but this time with her other hand.

'Please, bring me a mirror. I need to see.'

'There's nothing to see at the moment,' said the nurse. 'Your face is heavily bandaged, but in a few days, when the graft has taken, you'll be able to see more.'

'I don't care,' said Sarah. 'I need to see now!'

Reluctantly, the nurse agreed to Sarah's request and hurried back to her station to fetch a mirror. She returned a few minutes later, clutching a small mirror that she had taken from her handbag which she gingerly proceeded to place into Sarah's outstretched hand. The mirror was so small that Sarah initially struggled to position it so that she could see the full extent of her facial injuries, but after a short while eventually managed to catch sight of her profile. The nurse was, of course, right. Her head was so swathed in bandages that it was impossible to see the damage

that the geyser's boiling water had caused, but that didn't prevent
Sarah from asking,

'Oh my God! How much damage has been done?'

The nurse said nothing, but as she turned her face away
from Sarah's gaze and began busily re-arranging her dishevelled
bedding, it was clear to Sarah that her injuries were serious and
potentially highly disfiguring. Sarah wailed softly to herself and let
the mirror drop on to the bedclothes. Thankful of the opportunity
to extricate herself from the awkward situation, the nurse quickly
retrieved the mirror and then mumbling something about getting
a doctor's permission to give her some pain relief, returned to her
station to make a telephone call.

Left alone, a carrousel of questions and emotions began to
spiral uncontrollably, around and around, in Sarah's mind; each
one clamouring for her immediate attention and focus. Carlos was,
she now remembered, almost certainly dead, but as a feeling of
sadness began to well up inside her, the emotion was instantly and
almost rudely, pushed and jostled from the forefront of her mind
by another question, and then another; How badly had she been
burned? Where was Tom? Had he also been killed?

Sarah's chaotic train of thoughts and emotions was suddenly
interrupted by a voice from somewhere to her left.

'Ingleses?' asked the woman in the bed next to Sarah's.

Sarah simply nodded in reply.

'Cómo te quemas?' asked the woman.

Sarah understood perfectly what the woman was asking her,
but she was in too much pain to relate how she had sustained her
injuries to a complete stranger - so again, said nothing.

'Casa del fuego?' asked the woman, impatiently.

Sarah would have laughed out loud at the suggestion that
a house fire had caused her injuries, but for the pain in face.
Again, she said nothing, but this time raised her uninjured left

arm slightly in a gesture to indicate that the woman was correct. Thankfully, the return of the nurse to her bedside prevented any further interrogation from her fellow patient.

'I have brought you something for the pain and, if you feel up to it, there is someone who would like to speak to you.'

Sarah's brain went instantly into overdrive again. *A visitor! Who could it be? Is it Tom?*

Sarah nodded to the nurse and was about to ask who it was, when she suddenly heard a familiar voice say,

'Christ, Mum. What the hell have you been up to?'

The sound of her daughter's voice was better than any medication that the nurse could have given her and, in spite of the physical pain that she was suffering, Sarah smiled and immediately felt more secure and safe.

'My God, mother! You're dammed lucky to be alive. What the hell were you doing running around an erupting volcano? I thought you were supposed to be going to the farm to look for Tom, not wandering around the countryside with......'

Charlotte's voice trailed away when she realised that she was about to mention Carlos' name.

'Carlos,' croaked Sarah, finishing her daughter's sentence for her. 'It's ok, I know he's dead. He died in my arms.'

Charlotte hung her head slightly, and in an attempt to change the subject then said, 'Thank God Pedro was there to save you, or you, too, would have been killed.'

'Pedro saved me?' said Sarah, suddenly realising that the incomprehensible words that were being spoken to her as she was carried from the plaza must have been Pedro's.

'Yes, he carried you from the danger area and then drove you in the back of his lorry to the hospital in Santa Cruz, from where you were immediately air lifted by helicopter to the mainland.'

'And Tom?' asked Sarah. 'What about Tom?'

'Don't worry, Mum. He's safe and sound, but still on La Palma, helping with the evacuation following the second eruption.'

'Second eruption? What second eruption?'

But before Charlotte could answer, the stupefying effects of the morphine injection that the nurse had administered a moment earlier took hold and Sarah fell rapidly into a deep sleep.

Once certain that her mother was fast asleep and couldn't hear her, Charlotte asked, 'How bad is her face?' to the nurse, who had remained at Sarah's bed side waiting for the morphine to take effect.

'She has had the best care possible.' replied the nurse. 'Her doctor is one of the best plastic surgeons in all of Spain and if anyone can repair the damage to your mother's face, he can.'

Although Charlotte felt reassured by the nurse's reply, she could not help wondering how her mother would cope with what could well be a life changing injury and what, given her separation from Tom, the future would now hold for her. And then, somewhat selfishly perhaps, began to consider what life would be like for her – with the likelihood of having to run her business and, at the same time, care for her mother, now a distinct possibility.

Chapter 35

Funacaliente, La Palma

Day 6

When news of the tsunami and the death and destruction that it had caused on Tenerife and neighbouring islands reached Maria, Tom and the professor later that day, all three were still camped on a small hill just outside of Funacaliente. As their helicopter had been seconded by the Spanish Air Force to assist in the rescue mission underway on neighbouring islands, they were effectively marooned there for the time being. No one spoke; they simply sat and stared at the devastated town below, each deep in their own thoughts.

The town was now completely deserted and, although the southerly direction of the blast from the eruption had had no significant impact on the town's buildings, everywhere, as far as the eye could see, was coated in a thick layer of grey volcanic dust from the ash plume after it had collapsed. The once verdant and green countryside with its numerous banana plantations and lemon groves now resembled a lunar landscape and it was immediately apparent that life in the area would never be quite the same again.

Maria's thoughts were focused on what had happened to her sister, Consuela. As she had no way of knowing if her text had reached her in time, she couldn't be sure if Consuela was alive or dead and as she sat silently, fearing the worse, the professor, sensing Maria's concern about her sister's safety, gently placed his arm around her slender shoulders and drew her close to his body, softly whispering into her ear, 'I'm sure she'll be alright.'

Maria simply nodded in reply, but she knew, as did the professor, that the chances of her having survived were slim.

Tom's thoughts, too, were focused elsewhere. He couldn't be certain that the two people that he had seen in the plaza were Sarah and Carlos, but it had certainly looked like them. And if it had been them, he wondered how on Earth they could have survived the carnage that had ravaged the town and the surrounding area? But if they had, where were they now?

The professor was also deep in thought as he held Maria close. Over the last few days his affection for her had slowly, but inexorably, grown and, for the first time in more years than he could recall, he found himself thinking about what it would be like to share his life with someone else; someone as brave and beautiful as Maria. There could be no doubt that she was his intellectual equal - although he would never admit to that – and she also shared his passion for volcanology. But, more importantly, she was the first woman that he had ever met who seemed to be totally accepting of his curt and frequently intolerant manner and, dare he think it, the first woman who actually seemed to enjoy being in his company – irrespective of his mood. Maria was, he thought to himself, as he held her tighter and felt the heat radiating from her body, the perfect woman for him and, once this was all over, he silently vowed to himself, he would let her know just how much he felt for her.

Chapter 36

London

Two years later

It was late September when Tom received a letter from Maria telling him about her sister's wedding to Gomez and tentatively asking if he, and Sarah, would like to attend.

'Sarah,' he shouted, 'we've been invited to a wedding.'

'Whose wedding and when is it?' she replied.

'It's Maria's sister, Consuela. She's marrying the police man who was with her when the tsunami struck Tenerife.'

'Will the wedding be in the Canaries or on the Spanish mainland?'

Tom hesitated slightly before replying, as he knew his wife would not welcome what he was about to say.

'It's on ......'

But before he could complete his sentence, Sarah came into the lounge and said,

'It's on La Palma, isn't it?'

'Er, yes,' he replied.

'Don't worry, I'm over the worst of it now and I think I'm up to returning to La Palma.' But as she spoke, her hand moved automatically towards the wrinkled, red skin on the side of her face where, in spite of the skin grafts, the scarring caused by the boiling water from the erupting geyser was still partially visible.

'If you're sure,' said Tom.

'Yes, positive. Book the flights. When is it, anyway?'

'In two months' time. Maria said we can stay with her and the professor at their house on El Heirro, and then fly over to La Palma from there.'

'At Maria's and the professor's house you say. It sounds to me like they're an item,' said Sarah, smiling at Tom.

'From the letter it would seem to be that way, although I always suspected there was something brewing between them.'

'But didn't she have a boyfriend who died during the eruption on Cumbre Veija?'

'Yes, but there was always a sort of intangible chemistry between her and the professor. I noticed it on several occasions in the days leading up to the eruption. She clearly admired and respected him as an academic, but there was always something else, bubbling away under the surface and ready to erupt.'

Tom inwardly congratulated himself on his unintended pun and thought how the professor would have liked it, but not necessarily shown that he had found it amusing. But then he looked away and instantly felt decidedly uncomfortable when he saw the now pained expression on Sarah's face. Volcanic eruptions had left her scarred both physically and mentally, in spite of what she'd said only moments ago, and as soon as he'd said it, he wished that he hadn't.

'Older man syndrome, I suspect.' said Sarah, immediately noticing Tom's embarrassment and realising that he regretted his remark.

'Maybe it was. Certainly, the professor never gave any indication that he harboured feelings for her when I was with the two of them. He was always too focused on when, and how, that bloody volcano was going to erupt, so I suspect you're right – perhaps she was infatuated with him, rather than him with her,

but then again, I might be wrong. The professor is undoubtedly
a complex character and who knows, maybe his intellectual
superiority is all just a façade and beneath it, hidden from public
view, is a red hot Latin love machine ready to erupt.'

Tom smiled to himself as he imagined the professor dressed
in skin tight black trousers and a voluminous white cotton shirt,
strumming a guitar and singing a Spanish love ballad beneath
Maria's balcony.

'Or, if you like,' Tom continued, 'rather than stay at Maria's,
we could book a room at Granja en los Pinos. It would be good to
return to the old farm and see how the new owners are faring. The
estate agent told me that they have opened a Bed and Breakfast to
cater for walkers doing the new volcano trek that the tourist board
have set up since the eruption. Apparently it's been completely
rebuilt and even hooked up to the mains water and electricity
supply, so it should be a bit more comfortable than when we lived
there.'

Instantly, and for the second time in as many minutes, Tom
wished he hadn't said anything, but was quite taken aback when
Sarah replied,

'Ah, but we had the true rural experience and, hard though
it was, it was an experience worth having. The new owners will
never know what it's like to wash clothes by hand in a galvanised
tub with the sun beating down on your back and flies crawling up
your nose.'

Tom didn't say anything, but was secretly pleased that Sarah
had some small, but nevertheless seemingly positive memories
of their time in the finca, or at least he hoped they were positive
ones.

'Plus,' said Tom, buoyed by Sarah's apparent positivity, 'since
returning from hiding in the hills once all the fuss had died down,
I believe Daisy has made herself very much at home with the new

people and is eating them out of house and home.'

'I always knew that dog's love was one hundred per cent cupboard love.' said Sarah, smiling slightly as she recalled memories of chasing Daisy out of the finca's kitchen with a broom when she had found her with her head in a bin, stealing scraps one morning.

'You're probably right, but it would be good to see her again and maybe we could bring her back to England with us. I'm sure she'd love our new home in Norfolk - with all its modern conveniences,' added Tom.

'Yes,' said Sarah, 'and no earthquakes or volcanic eruptions.'

'Yes, nothing major to worry about in good. Nelson's county. Just the odd bit of coastal erosion and the occasional storm surge.'

'You are joking, aren't you?'

'Well......,' said Tom, hesitantly.

Sensing his uncertainty, Sarah repeated her question, slightly more vociferously this time.

'Please tell me you're not serious, Tom. I've had enough natural disasters to last me a life time and I don't want any more, thank you very much.'

'Don't panic,' said Tom. 'I've done my research this time and you can rest assured that the small market town of North Walsham is a hazard free zone; trust me,' and then continued, 'As far as I am aware, the only real danger that North Norfolk has to offer is being mown down by one of the region's many elderly residents on their mobility scooters.'

'You'd better be right,' said Sarah, and then, after a moment's contemplation, added,

'And how do you feel about returning to teaching after so long?'

'No problem whatsoever,' said Tom enthusiastically. 'Teaching at one of the country's top independent schools will be an absolute pleasure after my time in the State sector. No interfering Ofsted Inspectors - and no half - witted political initiatives to deal with. Just teaching. Bliss!'

'And what if it doesn't work out?' asked Sarah.

'In that case,' replied Tom, 'I'll spend my time giving lectures to WI groups.'

'About what?'

'Oh, how about, *'Lemon growing for beginners'* or, *'What to do if an earthquake strikes or a volcano erupts.''*

'Very droll,' said Sarah, 'I'm sure the twin set and pearl brigade of North Norfolk will lap it up!'

'Anyway,' said Tom, 'are you sure about a return to the island?'

'Yes, I'm fine with going back to La Palma, and I don't mind staying at Granja en los Pinos again, but I certainly don't wish to go back to Funacaliente. It holds too many bad memories for me.'

'I understand completely,' said Tom. 'Carlos and I became really close after you had gone back to England and I miss his company and friendship a great deal too.'

Sarah didn't reply. She simply stared out of the window of their daughter's flat and wondered if one day she would eventually reveal to Tom the ulterior motive she had had for returning to La Palma. *No,* she thought, *some things are best left unsaid and Tom need never know the real reason for her return. Carlos would remain her guilty secret and her 'Shirley Valentine' moment would go with her to the grave.*

'But we could visit Pedro's grave and the monument that has been built outside the town to commemorate all those who lost their lives,' said Tom.

'Yes, after picking me up and carrying me out of the plaza after the fountain blew, I feel I should pay my respects to him and it would also be good to see the memorial.'

'Apparently, the town as we knew it has long gone and the

surrounding countryside is much changed. Since the eruption wiped out most of the agriculture in the area, the town was deserted by the locals and the only people who pass that way now are walkers and tourists hoping to see the geyser spout.'

'It's a terrible shame,' said Sarah, 'but it was always on the cards I believe.'

'Yes, I remember Carlos telling me a few days before it erupted how long overdue an eruption of Teneguia was, but no one could ever have expected that it would be such a violent one or that it would cause such a devastating tsunami. Well, apart from the professor and Maria, of course. They knew it was going to happen, but just didn't have the time to issue a warning.'

'So, shall I book the tickets?' asked Tom.

'Yes, do, and book a few nights at Granje en los Pinos whilst you're at it, too.'

As Tom left the room to go and make the bookings, he couldn't help but allow himself a small smile, not just because they were returning to somewhere which he still, in spite of all that had happened there, held dear, but also because, at last, it seemed that Sarah was beginning to lay to rest some of the demons that had haunted her for the last two years.

Chapter 37

Granje en los Pinos, La Palma

Tom and Sarah stood on the ridge which overlooked their former home and were amazed at how different everything now seemed since the eruption. The finca was hardly recognisable, but clearly much improved, with new walls made from local stone, hardwood windows and even a new roof. The building had been extended into the area where the old barn had once stood, presumably to provide accommodation for guests, and what had once been the finca's kitchen, was now a covered patio area with recliners, ideal for relaxing after a hard day's trek in the mountains with, of course, a gin and tonic and a good book. Tom squirmed slightly when he caught sight of Sarah looking longingly at the addition of the patio and positively wriggled with embarrassment when two guests appeared carrying drinks and reading material.

Noticing Tom's apparent discomfort, Sarah decided to have some fun at his expense and said, 'Is that the sound of ice chinking in their glasses? My God, I do believe it is! Don't tell me our accommodation has a fridge.'

Tom smiled and held his hands up in a gesture of surrender.

'You win. It's now what I would have liked it to have been when we lived here but….'

Sarah finished his sentence for him, 'A volcanic eruption got in the way of your plans.'

'Yes, something like that,' he replied, looking wistfully at the distant Atlantic Ocean.

But the biggest change of all to their former home was the addition of a swimming pool. Tom and Sarah stared, not quite believing their eyes, at the aquamarine rectangle of sparkling clear water which now occupied where a lemon grove had once been.

'You know, Sarah, when I look at that pool, I could almost cry when I think about how precious and hard to come by water was when we were here,'

'Well, it looks like one positive thing has come out of the eruption,' said Sarah. 'The rupturing of the rock aquifer further up the mountain has clearly solved the age old problem of securing a water supply for homes on the ridge, but it seems a shame that it's no longer being used to raise crops.'

'Little chance of that,' said Tom, as he turned to survey the lunar like landscape which now surrounded their former farm.

The steep slopes above and below Granje en los Pinos were no longer clad in sweet smelling pine and juniper trees, and the lemon and olive groves, which Tom had so carefully tendered during his time at the farm, were now all gone too. The landscape was almost completely devoid of any vegetation and the mountainside was cloaked, instead, in a sterile layer of grey ash and blood red clumps of cinder. Without any trees, the chaffinches had long since disappeared as, too, had the buzzards which, before the eruption, would soar skywards each morning on the thermals rising from the Llanos Valley floor and spend the day slowly circling high above the finca, looking for prey. And the wind ascending from the valley floor also no longer bore the heady smell of resin and herbs that Tom and Sarah had so enjoyed when sitting, late at night, on the veranda of their farm. Now the winds only carried the very faint odour of sulphur and chlorine; a smell which made Tom shiver slightly as it evoked memories of his journey into Funacaliente that fateful morning; a journey that heralded the end of life as they knew it on the ridge.

'Nothing will ever grow on these slopes,' said Tom sadly, 'Certainly not in our lifetime, at least.'

'But it once did,' said Sarah, 'and who knows, maybe one day, in the future, it will again.'

'Perhaps,' said Tom, 'but I'm not so sure. But, let's not dwell any longer on what was once here; we have a wedding to go to, and unless we get a move on we're going to be late.'

However, as they turned to walk back down the slope to their accommodation, a familiar sounding whimper from behind them caused them to stop dead in their tracks. And, as they turned around, they saw Daisy, wagging her tail furiously at the sight of Tom, and creating, as all Border collies do at times of high excitement, a small puddle of urine behind her. But, most amazingly of all, she was surrounded by a litter of her pups.

'My god dog,' said Tom, 'I can see you found something to occupy your time whilst up in the mountains. And I thought it was only chasing rabbits and pinching food that you were interested in. My, oh my, you little rascal, you.'

'You see,' said Sarah, with a broad smile on her face, 'life in these mountains does go on, after all.'

The End

Acknowledgements

I should like to thank my wife, Sharon, and my daughters, Hannah and Meg, for their constant support, encouragement and patience whilst writing this book and also my brother, Andrew, for giving me the inspiration to start writing it in the first place.

About the author

After graduating from the University of Plymouth, Peter Bennett has spent most of his working life teaching Geography at a grammar school in Colchester, Essex, where he still lives, with his wife, two children and Ruby, his faithful Border collie. He recently retired from full-time teaching in order to devote more time to writing and landscape painting and is currently working on his second novel, 'Tunnel Vision' which is scheduled for publication early next year.